THE
KINGS COPSE
KILLER

An enthralling murder mystery with a twist

FRANCES LLOYD

DI Jack Dawes Mystery Series Book 10

Joffe Books, London
www.joffebooks.com

First published in Great Britain in 2022

Cover art by Dee Dee Book Covers

ISBN: 978-1-80405-549-6

No one is good; no one is evil; everyone is both, in the same way and in different ways . . .

Paul Gaugin 1848–1903

CHAPTER ONE

Zizi Starr drove a fluorescent yellow Mini. It was covered in flower decals, signs of the zodiac and branded *The Galaxy Boutique* — a mobile advertisement for her shop. She sold quirky jewellery, aromatherapy oils and candles, mystic stones and healing crystals — cool stuff for cool people. She also read horoscopes and tarot cards based on a loosely acquired knowledge of astrology. But despite her claims to clairvoyance, when she set out on that sunny afternoon in August, she'd had no premonition of the gruesome, sickening horror that was about to engulf her.

It was ten minutes to two and Zizi was sitting at a table in Chez Carlene, a French bistro in the trendy food and drink quarter of Kings Richington. She was wearing a breezy print blouse with a long, flowing skirt and a wide-brimmed hat with sunflowers on it. She favoured clothes that made a statement — designs that said something about her lifestyle. The crossbody bag and hippy shades completed the look. She'd been there since one o'clock, nibbling bread dipped in aioli and waiting for her friend Allegra to join her for lunch. They'd been friends since they were children. Allegra's mother had died when she was five, and Zizi had lost her father at around the same age. They used to complain that

1

they had only one set of parents between them. Then, when Zizi's mother died in a car accident in the Italian Alps and Allegra's lawyer father, Grafton Parnell, had succumbed to heart failure, they had declared themselves mature orphans and become even closer. Allegra's apparently random wedding to Brian Roberts, which she flippantly described as a "starter marriage", had had no impact on their friendship whatsoever — neither positive nor negative.

When Allegra still hadn't put in an appearance by two o'clock and all Zizi's calls had gone straight to voicemail, she became slightly concerned. Allegra was never late. As a successful divorce lawyer with a heavy workload, she kept to a tight schedule. Since Grafton Parnell's demise, only weeks ago, the law firm of Parnell & Parnell in which Allegra had been a partner had become her sole responsibility, along with all the staff. She worked hard – but she still found time to play hard.

Zizi decided to drive the ten miles out into the country to Allegra's house in Richington Mallet and find out what had happened to delay her. She parked her Mini in front of the ivy-clad barn conversion that Allegra Parnell shared with "starter husband" Brian. Allegra's ostentatious flamered sports car was parked in the drive, so she hadn't yet left home. Even before Zizi climbed out of her Mini, she could see that the heavy oak front door was ajar, which was unlike her security-conscious friend.

She walked up and pushed it open. 'Ally, where are you, you dozy tart? You've left your door open. We were supposed to be meeting for—' She stepped inside then screamed, nonstop, for a full half-minute.

* * *

Sergeant Norman Parsloe was on the desk at Kings Richington police station when the emergency call came through. The member of the public on the other end was clearly distraught, and he was having trouble understanding her. 'Please try to calm down, madam. Tell me your name and where you are and I'll send some officers to help you.' After he'd ended the call, having assured the lady that the police would soon be with her, he looked on the computer to see who was nearest in the area car. He radioed them.

'Walker, Johnson, there's something weird going on at a house in Richington Mallet.' He gave PC "Johnny" Johnson the address. 'It's probably nothing — the lady was hysterical — kept going on about all the blood and a man with no head.'

'Sounds like she's on something, to me, Sarge,' suggested Constable Walker. 'Did you get her name?'

Parsloe looked at his notes. 'Zizi Starr.'

'Well, that explains it,' grinned Constable Johnson. 'She owns that wacky shop in the high street. It's full of psychedelic bollocks. She's probably been sniffing her own joss sticks.'

'Well, get over there and sort her out. Call an ambulance if you think she needs it. Report back when you've contained the situation.'

In the area car, speeding towards Richington Mallet, Constable Walker asked, 'What was the address again, Johnny?'

'Oak Lodge. It's one of those new, classy barn conversions down by the river. It's virtually crime-free, that village. No burglaries or assaults, just lost cats and stolen garden gnomes. Why? Do you know it?'

'No,' replied Walker. 'I've never been to Richington Mallet.'

They spotted Zizi's car as soon as they turned into the lane. 'Bloody hell!' exclaimed Johnson. 'Fancy driving around in a motor like that. It wouldn't do if you had a hangover.' They pulled up alongside the Mini and climbed out, putting on their flat peaked caps.

Zizi was sitting in her car with all the doors locked. When the officers approached, she wound down her window, but all she could do was point and croak, 'In there. They're in there.'

'OK, madam,' said Johnson. This lady wasn't "on" anything – she was severely traumatized. Her makeup was smeared all over her face, her eyes were red and swollen and she was trembling. 'You just sit there, Ms Starr. Leave it to us, now.'

It was the abattoir smell that hit them, even before they were inside. Pungent, metallic and slightly sweet. There was blood everywhere — up the walls, over the floor, spattered on the hall mirror and sprinkled over a vase of white roses, giving them a bizarre, speckled effect, like tiger lilies. A grisly trail of blood from the body of a woman lying face down halfway up the stairs had congealed into a pool on the oak flooring below. She'd been shot in the back. Another body, a man, was slumped against the kitchen door. A shot at point-blank range had effectively blasted his head from his shoulders and splattered his brains and pieces of his skull in all directions.

Wayne Walker took one look and dashed outside, where he threw up, violently, on the step. Johnny Johnson grabbed his radio. 'Sarge, we've got a major incident and a bad one. Two people dead, killed most probably with a double-barrelled shotgun. I reckon this is one for the Murder Investigation Team.'

* * *

The incident room of the MIT was spectacularly short of incidents. The whiteboard was blank and detectives were going through cold, unsolved cases. Advances in forensics, technology and information-sharing capabilities meant that cold cases were reviewed in order to determine the potential for further investigation and a possible resolution. Many of the murders dated back several years and, in some cases, the police hadn't even found a body. Not much to go on, but Chief Superintendent Garwood, the head of MIT, liked to report to the commander that he was giving the taxpayer value for money, even when things were quiet.

Detective Inspector Jack Dawes was hoping for an uneventful afternoon, so that he might go home at a reasonable hour to watch the rugby on the television. His misaligned features bore witness to his own rugby-playing days, when he was still young and fit enough to get stuck in with the pack. Nowadays, the only game he played with a pack was poker. When Parsloe appeared, looking grim, he suspected his hopes of knocking off early were under serious threat.

'Norman, what can we do for you?' asked DS Mike "Bugsy" Malone, biting into a jumbo iced bun. It had only been two hours since he'd had a full canteen lunch, but already he reckoned he could feel his blood sugar dropping. 'I can tell from your face you haven't come up here to tell us that a funny thing happened to you on the way to the station.'

'You're needed out at Richington Mallet. My officers were called out to a major incident — a nasty one. Two people killed with a shotgun. Blood all over, apparently. Very messy, according to Constable Johnson. Constable Walker's still throwing up.'

'It'd better not be all over Big Ron's crime scene or the lad will get the sharp edge of her tongue,' said Bugsy, who had himself been on the receiving end of this many times.

"Big Ron" was the affectionate nickname the team had for the pathologist, Dr Veronica Hardacre. She was not only big in stature but had a superb scientific brain. Her appearance was similarly impressive. Tall and muscular with bristling black eyebrows and a matching moustache, Big Ron did not suffer fools, nor did she tolerate impatient senior police officers who asked "damn fool" questions and expected her to speculate about important issues before she'd had time to evaluate them properly.

Jack reached for his coat. 'Right, I want Doctor Hardacre and a full SOCO team out there straight away before random people start contaminating everything and the blasted media get hold of the story. Bugsy, you're with me.'

Detective Constables Gemma Fox and Aled Williams looked up, hopefully. Trawling through cold, long-abandoned cases was not the most interesting of jobs. Jack took pity on them. 'OK, you two. You'd better attend as well. There'll be statements to take while memories are still fresh.'

'And wading through blood and guts will be a good experience for you,' quipped Bugsy. Detective Sergeant Malone knew all about experience, having been a copper for more years than he cared to remember. He'd recently had a spell of Acting Detective Inspector while Jack had been on holiday. It had been challenging and he'd earned a commendation, but he was much happier as Jack's wingman, especially at times like this.

* * *

'Good of you to turn up, DI Dawes.' Dr Hardacre had arrived first, together with her assistant, Marigold Catwater. 'I trust we haven't disturbed your afternoon nap.' They were both wearing full protective clothing and it would have been difficult to tell them apart except tiny Marigold was half the size of Big Ron. The pathologist was at work, meticulously analysing the crime scene, which was now cordoned off by blue police tape. Clenched-faced but steady, Miss Catwater was following her around with tamper-evident containers, various disposable tweezers and scissors and a voice recorder.

'Don't touch that!' Dr Hardacre yelled through her mask at DS Malone, who looked as if he was about to pick up the victim's handbag. 'Yes, I know you're wearing gloves, but I'd prefer it if as few people as possible handle anything in the room. The team will need to check the bag for fingerprints in case this was a robbery gone wrong. But somehow, I don't think so.'

'Do we have the identities of the victims?' asked Jack. He understood why PC Walker had vomited — smells affected him the same way, never mind the carnage all around them.

'Yes, sir.' DC Fox consulted her notes. 'They are Allegra Parnell and her husband, Brian Roberts. I got that much from Zizi Starr before they took her away in an ambulance. She discovered the bodies. She said she was alerted to a problem when Ms Parnell didn't turn up for a lunch date, so she drove here and this is what she found. They have apparently been close friends since they were children and she's very upset. I'll get a full statement from her when she's feeling better.'

Jack turned cautiously to Dr Hardacre. 'Any initial thoughts, Doctor?'

'A few. This is really a job for Ballistics but it's fairly obvious the injuries were inflicted using a shotgun — most probably a twelve-bore but not a semi-automatic. We didn't find any ejected cartridges, so I assume they are still in the chamber, unless the perpetrator has removed them manually. Given the nature of the wounds, I'd say the woman was shot first, running away from the gunman who was standing in the doorway. She got halfway up the stairs when he fired. The central mass of shotgun pellets tends to break up at around the two-metre mark so you get the widespread pattern of individual holes that you see here, but no discernible central hole.'

DC Williams was fascinated. 'That's why there are all those spots on the walls around her?'

'Correct, Constable. A lot depends on the characteristics of the weapon involved. Forensic ballistics experts can carry out tests to discover whether a suspect weapon was responsible for this particular pattern and from what distance the discharge was likely to have occurred. The only problem with that, of course, is that we haven't yet found the weapon. Uniform and SOCOs are still searching.'

'What about this poor devil, Doc?' Bugsy indicated the headless body slumped against the door.

Dr Hardacre was, as always, dispassionate. 'This man was almost certainly shot at point-blank range. I'd say fifteen to thirty centimetres. At this distance, the pellets in the cartridge don't have time to spread so they enter the head as a single mass. A large volume of gas enters the cranium at the same time and as you will observe, the effect is one of massive destruction. Pieces of skull and brain tissue have been spread over a wide area. Determining the point of contact will require meticulous gathering of skull fragments and attempting to reconstruct the head in order to find the hole. As I say, this is really a job for Forensic Ballistics.'

'Time of death, Doctor?' Jack knew he was pushing his luck.

She pursed her lips. 'I'd say sometime between seven and midnight yesterday, but don't hold me to it. I'll know more after the post-mortem. Now, please will you bugger off and let me get on with my job?'

CHAPTER TWO

The whiteboard in the incident room was filling up rapidly with names, times and the little they knew about the murders. It had also been populated with photos of the two corpses, their locations and a wedding photo of Allegra Parnell and Brian Roberts when Brian had still had a head.

'OK, team,' said Dawes. 'What do we think happened here? Remember the three essentials — Means — Motive — Opportunity.'

'The means is pretty obvious,' said Malone. 'Ballistics have described the potential weapon as a long-barrelled, probably smoothbore firearm designed to shoot a straight-walled cartridge. SOCOs didn't find any spent cartridges so the killer didn't eject them. They could still be in the gun, wherever it is.'

'Maybe the killer took it away and dumped it somewhere,' suggested DC Fox. 'The River Richington is close by.'

'Would he or she have had the presence of mind to do something that rational after slaughtering two people?' asked DC Williams.

'Self-preservation is instinctive, son. His first thought, seconds after he did it would have been, "How can I get away with it?"' said Bugsy.

'And I'll bet you next month's salary, the killer was a bloke,' added Jack.

'Are you saying that a woman wouldn't be capable of doing this, sir?' asked DC Fox.

'No, Gemma, I'm saying that most women would find a more considered, less frenzied way of getting rid of two people, whatever the motive. They'd think it through and weigh up the consequences, not come in blasting away like Butch Cassidy.'

'What about opportunity?' asked Bugsy. 'SOCOs said they didn't find any evidence of a break-in, so how did the killer get in?'

'From what I was able to get from Zizi, she found the door ajar, which she said was most unusual, as Allegra was very security conscious,' reported Gemma. 'Apparently, she only bought the barn conversion recently and hadn't yet got around to having CCTV and burglar alarms fitted, but it was to be a priority.'

'So we have to assume that either Brian or Allegra let the killer in,' said Bugsy.

'Did we find any tyre tracks?' asked Jack. 'The killer must have come in some sort of vehicle. Oak Lodge is right out in the country. He would hardly have risked walking through Richington Mallet carrying a shotgun, then walking back covered in blood.'

''Fraid not, guv,' said Bugsy. 'There was a heavy down-pour of rain during the night. Uniform taped off the drive but by then, Zizi Starr's Mini had driven over anything that might have been useful and traffic was still churning up the mud down the lane.'

'Well, she wasn't to know she was about to walk in and find two dead bodies,' mused Jack.

'How about this for a motive?' offered Aled. 'Hubby — that's Brian — comes home and finds his wife, Allegra, having it away with another bloke. We don't know who he is but we could maybe find out. Mad with jealousy, Brian fetches his shotgun, meaning to dispatch both of them. Boyfriend legs it, so hubby shoots wife, who's running away up the stairs. Then, filled with remorse, he sticks the gun in his mouth and blows his head off. It's well documented in crimes of passion that suicide often follows a murder.'

The team looked at him in wonder for several moments.

'Just one or two flaws in your argument, Aled,' said Jack. 'Firstly, there's no gun cabinet in the house and no indication that Roberts ever applied for a gun licence, owned a shotgun or knew how to load and fire one. Secondly, if she was caught "having it away" with a boyfriend, how come she was fully clothed and running upstairs and not down?'

'And we won't go into the clichéd arguments about how he'd have needed to have arms long enough to pull the trigger with the barrel in his mouth,' added Gemma.

'OK,' said Bugsy. 'Let's assume for the sake of argument that your theory is right, son. Having blown his own head off, how did Brian manage to get up, dispose of the gun, then sit back down again?'

'Are you sure you're cut out for this job, Aled?' asked Gemma.

Aled made a rude, one-fingered gesture at her. 'I didn't say it was foolproof, did I? I was just tossing around an idea, backed up by past case studies.'

'Well, I'd toss that one away, if I were you,' advised Gemma.

'Maybe Zizi Whatsname took the gun away before she called us. Did we search her car?' Aled was trying to regain some credibility. 'She could have guessed who did it and she's covering for him.'

Gemma sighed, wearily. 'Aled, she was Allegra's closest, dearest, lifelong friend. If she'd known who killed her, she'd have ripped off his balls then shoved his shotgun where the sun don't shine.'

'Are we even sure the dead bloke was Brian Roberts?' suggested Aled. 'After all, his head was missing. Zizi might have just assumed it was him. Maybe it was the boyfriend and Brian is still alive.'

11

'Maybe,' said Gemma. 'But DNA doesn't assume anything. It was definitely Brian. Get a grip, Aled. You're chasing chimeras instead of looking at the facts.'

Jack intervened before everyone completely lost the plot. 'Instead of speculating on a possible motive, we need lifestyle information about our victims to throw up a more probable motive. Do we know what Brian and Allegra did for a living?'

Clive, the digital forensics specialist, or "techie geek" as he was known to the team, had done some digging. 'Brian James Roberts, aged thirty-eight, taught music at Richington Comprehensive for the last fifteen years, sir. His only job since leaving university. No close relatives that I could find. Married Allegra Parnell shortly after they both graduated. Financially stable but not well-off. Drove an old dark blue Ford Focus, acquired second-hand. It's still in the garage at Oak Lodge.'

'Just an ordinary, OK kind of guy, then,' commented Aled.

'Yep. No form but questioned by police two years ago, along with a lot of other people, after one of his star music pupils, Kirsty Jackson, disappeared. She's never been found and the case remains open on MISPER records for yearly review.'

'So what about Allegra, Clive? What do we know about her?'

'She wasn't what I would consider an obvious match for Brian Roberts, sir, and she rarely used his name, but then again, I'm not a relationship guru. I've never been able to fathom what attracts people to other people. She was a solicitor in the law firm Parnell & Parnell specializing in divorce.'

'Just because she had a law degree, it doesn't mean she was smarter than everyone else,' observed Aled. 'After all, Gemma has one.' He ducked as she swiped at him with her ruler.

'She practised under the name Allegra Parnell,' continued Clive. 'The firm was started by her father, Grafton Parnell. He made her a partner soon after she joined. He recently died of a cardiac arrest, leaving her to run the firm. It's difficult to hack into any financial or personal information as she had it well protected, but she drove a snazzy Mazda sports car, less than a year old, and the house was in her name. No form but she was cautioned a couple of times demonstrating for various feminist issues while she was at university. No charges were brought.'

DC "Mitch" Mitchell, one of the older members of the team, had been listening intently. He pointed at the dead couple on the board. 'It seems to me, sir, that these two had very little in common, apart from the fact they were husband and wife.'

There were grunts of empathy around the room. 'Tell me about it,' muttered someone.

'Is it safe to assume that, as Big Ron said, the woman was shot first? Allegra was the target and poor old Brian was just collateral damage — wrong place, wrong time?'

'You could well be right, Mitch, but we mustn't lose sight of the possibility that it could have been the other way around. The killer came to shoot Brian but Allegra got in the way, so he had to dispatch her first.' Jack stood up. 'Right, folks, we need to gather some information but not tonight — it's getting late. First thing in the morning, Gemma, go and speak to Zizi Starr again. I understand she's back in her shop so you may be able to obtain a more coherent statement. Aled, I need you to visit Richington Comprehensive. Find out what kind of teacher Brian Roberts was and what his colleagues thought of him. DS Malone and I will interview the remaining staff at Parnell & Parnell.'

The briefing dispersed as everyone left to go home, ready for an early start the next day.

* * *

Zizi Starr had spent a sleepless night. She was in two minds about whether to reopen The Galaxy Boutique. She was scared — very scared. She lived in a tiny flat above the shop.

Despite alarms and CCTV all along the street outside, it wouldn't be difficult for someone to break in and do to her what he'd done to Allegra. She had more or less decided to close up the shop and go to stay with her cousin in Cornwall when the chimes over the door, placed there to maximize the flow of chi, announced the presence of DC Fox, who produced her warrant card. 'Can we have a chat, Ms Starr?'

'Hello, Constable Fox. Yes, I remember you from . . .' She paused, not wanting to recreate the ugly scene in her head. The trouble was that having seen it, in all its gory gruesomeness, she couldn't now unsee it.

'I'm sorry, I know this must be distressing and I'm sorry for your loss, but I need to ask you a few questions, Ms Starr.'

'Can I get you some tea, officer? I have chamomile, bergamot and lavender, lemongrass, acai berry—'

'No, I'm fine, thank you.' Gemma's cheeks puckered at the very thought. Why did people take a perfectly palatable beverage like tea and contrive to turn it into something that tasted like scented ditchwater? 'I believe you and Ms Parnell Roberts had been friends for a number of years.'

'Yes, since we were little. Hardly a day passed that we didn't speak or message each other.'

'I'm sorry, but I have to ask this — where were you between seven and midnight the day before you found her?'

'I was here, doing a stocktake until late. You can't surely believe that I killed Allegra and Brian? It's ludicrous—'

'Well, somebody did, Ms Starr, and in a very violent manner. Can you think of a reason why anyone might want to harm either of them?'

At this point, Gemma thought she saw a flicker of apprehension cross Zizi's face but she answered firmly. 'No. Not at all. They were a sweet couple. Everyone adored them.' She paused. 'How do you know Brian didn't shoot Allegra then turn the gun on himself?'

Gemma wasn't at liberty to divulge details of the missing shotgun or any other facts about the crimes. She'd been tasked with obtaining information, not providing it. 'Why would you think that? Did Mr Roberts have a motive for killing his wife?'

Zizi backed off. 'Not really. Allegra tended to have "liaisons", but they never lasted long and Brian was always too busy with his music to notice. He always claimed that Allegra had been the love of his life when they were at university. I'm not so sure that was the case recently, though. I only suggested it might have been Brian because you hear of such things, don't you?'

The interview continued for some minutes with Gemma making copious notes but nothing of any significance emerged. When she got up to leave, Zizi said, 'I'm thinking of taking a holiday, to help me get over this ghastly shock. I'm going to stay with my cousin in Truro.'

'Erm . . . I don't think that's a good idea, Ms Starr. You see, at the moment, you are what we call a "person of interest" since you were first on the scene. Please don't leave Kings Richington without notice.'

Zizi's face fell. 'But I have to get away, I don't feel safe here.'

Gemma picked up the flicker of apprehension again. 'Why is that? Have you any reason to believe you are in danger?'

Zizi retracted. 'No . . . no . . . not at all. It's fine. I'll stay here until you catch whoever did this awful thing.'

After Gemma had gone, Zizi packed a bag, locked the shop, set all the alarms and got into her car. The auspices were not good. Her tarot reading had given her Death, the four of Swords, the five of Swords, and the Knight of Swords, indicating a number of diabolical situations. She wasn't staying to be picked off at random. After all, she wasn't under arrest. The police could think what they liked.

* * *

When DC Williams arrived at Richington Comprehensive, he was immediately shown into the head teacher's study. Dr

Lambrick held a PhD in divinity and a firm conviction that every student in her school was bent on committing a deadly sin, the second her back was turned. It was, she believed, her job to prevent it and save their souls. When her mild-mannered, God-fearing music teacher had been found murdered in such a dreadful fashion, it had further reinforced her life-long belief that the devil lurks all around, lying in wait to pounce on any unwary victim.

'Constable Williams, please sit down.' She motioned him to an uncomfortable-looking chair on the opposite side of her large, ugly mahogany desk. 'I understand you're here about poor Mr Roberts. Do the police have any idea who did this terrible thing?'

'Not yet, Doctor Lambrick. It's early days and we're following several lines of enquiry. I understand Mr Roberts had been teaching here for some time.'

'That's correct. He joined us as a music teacher some fifteen years ago, then became head of music ten years later. He was an accomplished pianist, a skill he passed on to several fortunate students over the years. He will be greatly missed.'

So much for the virtual obituary, thought Aled. *Nothing there to inspire murder.* He needed to know something about the man's lifestyle. 'What about his private life, Doctor Lambrick? What can you tell me about that?'

She visibly recoiled. 'Nothing at all, officer. I make a point of never enquiring into the private lives of my staff. You can never tell what you might find. As long as they perform their teaching duties to the high standards this school has come to expect and don't do anything to bring it into disrepute, what they do in their spare time is their own business.'

Aled decided he was unlikely to gain anything useful from this paragon of virtue. She was a religious personification of the three wise monkeys. 'Do you think I might speak with some of Mr Roberts' colleagues?'

'Certainly, although I doubt if they will be able to tell you anything further.' She glanced at the huge clock on the wall that looked as if it had once belonged in St Pancras

Station. 'It's breaktime, so they'll be in the staff room. My school secretary will show you the way. Good day, Constable Williams, and may God help you find this killer before he breaks the fifth commandment yet again.'

The other teachers were vague about Brian Roberts. He appeared to be the original invisible man, going about his job in a bland, unremarkable way. Most of them thought music was a waste of teaching time, anyway. As the maths teacher put it, 'We've got our work cut out trying to teach the little buggers to read, write and count, never mind fannying about with musical instruments and rapping. They all want to be rock stars or YouTubers instead of getting a proper job. Roberts actively encouraged it.'

'There was that one girl, though,' recalled the English teacher. 'I've forgotten her name. It was about two years ago.'

'Kirsty Jackson,' offered the chemistry teacher. 'Only sixteen and already a brilliant young pianist — concert material, Brian said. She was his protégée. He'd arranged an exam that would have got her into a highly acclaimed music academy but she disappeared the night before. That was the most affected I ever saw him.'

'That's right. He was quite ill for a while. He'd put a lot of work into coaching her and she had certainly seemed very dedicated. Not the type of kid to push off to a music festival without telling anyone, for example, and just not come back.'

'Does anyone know what happened to her?' asked Aled.

'No. She just vanished off the face of the earth,' continued the chemistry teacher. 'Her parents were devastated. The police came and questioned us all, and Kirsty's friends, but she was never found. After that, Brian just got on with the job of day-to-day teaching.'

'D'you remember last year, when old Bri brought his wife to Open Day?' Mr Knobbs, the PE teacher, was posing by the water cooler in a superstar three-stripe tracksuit and trendy limited-edition trainers. He clearly fancied himself, and expected everyone else to do the same. 'Turned out he was married to that hot lawyer who's hyped on Twitter under

17

her handle @DivorceDiva. She was a real stunner. Who'd have thought it? He kept her well hidden, the crafty sod. She didn't seem to liven him up much, though. He was always a boring bastard.'

'Allegra Parnell, Brian Roberts' wife, was killed with him,' said Aled, solemnly. 'The police are investigating both murders.'

The PE teacher's laddish comments dried up instantly. Aled knew a self-obsessed idiot when he saw one, but even Knobbs knew when to shut up. 'Oh yeah. I remember seeing it on the news. Sorry. Bad business.'

Aled asked if he might have a few words with Brian's music students, with a teacher riding shotgun as a responsible adult. The kids all confirmed Mr Roberts was a really nice bloke — never shouted and was helpful if you were having problems. An ace pianist, too — he could play any tune you liked, even modern stuff. Nobody remembered Kirsty Jackson.

Driving back to the station, Aled wondered if Roberts had had a 'thing' for Kirsty, perhaps got too fond of her. Maybe she had rejected his advances and in a moment of frustration, he killed her. It wouldn't be the first time something like that had happened — an older bloke obsessed with a pretty, gifted teenager. What if, for example, the girl's father had jumped to that conclusion and decided to punish Roberts? But he wouldn't have left it two years, would he? Unless he'd only just found out. Maybe someone should interview the parents. He'd mention it in his report to the boss.

CHAPTER THREE

The law firm, Parnell & Parnell, was something of a misnomer now that both Parnells were dead. Jack and Bugsy had made an appointment to visit out of courtesy, although a police investigation into a double murder took priority over folk who were just looking to escape from a miserable marriage. The office and its staff were predictably sombre, feeling the loss of first Grafton, now Allegra. They were met by the office manager, Jane Shaw.

'You're here about Ms Parnell. What a dreadful thing to have happened. Do the police have any idea who's responsible?'

'We're following a number of leads, madam,' replied Malone, 'but we're hoping you can give us some background information concerning Ms Parnell's clients.'

'Well, she'd taken on Mr Parnell's cases as well as her own. She was gradually getting up to speed with his workload. You do realize that I can't allow you to look through any of our clients' details without a warrant?'

'Did she have any especially disaffected clients?' asked Dawes.

'You mean anyone pissed off enough to want her dead?' she asked, bluntly. 'She handled divorce cases, Inspector, and she was very good at it. By definition, it's an emotive subject and even under the new no-fault legislation, people don't normally go into it or come out of it feeling joyful, but I don't think anyone had actually threatened to kill her.'

'There must have been some clients who found themselves considerably worse off as a result of her representation, not to say potless,' said Malone.

'Oh yes. Allegra was very good at extracting cash out of people. She took a pride in getting a good settlement for her clients and she made sure she came out of it well herself. She didn't undertake legal aid work. Her clients were mostly members of wealthy families.'

'Did she only accept women clients?' asked Malone.

'Not at all. She handled all aspects of divorce law, particularly those involving hidden assets, valuable or complex corporate structures and unusual legal issues. She acted equally for those seeking to protect their wealth and those fighting to claim a share of it.'

'Did you like her, Ms Shaw?' asked Dawes.

'Not particularly. She was the boss — whether I liked her or not was irrelevant. I felt sorry for her poor husband, though. He was a lovely guy, kind and warm. It said on the news that he was shot, too.'

Dawes nodded. 'That's right. Why did you feel sorry for Brian Roberts?'

'Allegra treated him appallingly, in my opinion. She called him her "starter husband" and said he was approaching his "sell-by date". She boasted that compared to her, he only earned a pittance as a teacher, so she never shared anything financial with him such as a joint bank account or investments — and the house was in her sole name.'

'Some might say that was sensible, especially with her experience of expensive divorces.'

Jane lowered her voice. 'It wasn't just that. She humiliated him with other men. I don't know why I'm whispering — she made no attempt to keep her affairs a secret. Everybody knew.'

'Did she have a lover at the time she was killed?' asked Malone.

Jane looked thoughtful. 'Yes, but for some reason, she didn't make it public this time. We knew she was seeing someone that she described as "well fit", but she didn't say who he was. You don't think it was this man who shot them both, do you?'

'It's impossible to say, Ms Shaw, and we try not to speculate, but we'll certainly keep an open mind during the investigation.' Malone handed her a card. 'If you think of anything else, please give us a ring.'

After they'd gone, Jane went into the ladies' and permitted herself some private tears of grief.

* * *

Driving back to the station, Jack and Bugsy were talking over what Jane Shaw had told them. 'If it wasn't for the fact that the shotgun was missing,' said Bugsy, 'I'd be inclined to suspect young Aled's scenario was a possibility.' He pulled a sausage roll out of his pocket, brushed off the fluff and bit it in half.

'You mean Brian Roberts finally got fed up with being treated like a "starter husband", but didn't want anyone else to have Allegra, so he shot her then committed suicide?' Jack said. 'But that suggests someone showed up afterwards and took away the gun. Maybe the anonymous boyfriend?'

'Yeah. Although I can't see a bloke turning up expecting some illicit nookey, walking into a gory scene like that then just buggering off with the bloodstained gun, can you? Maybe Jane Shaw's suggestion was right — it was the boyfriend who did it.'

'Either way, we need to trace, identify and eliminate whoever he is. Get Clive onto it. He has weird and wonderful ways with TIE, most of which are illegal, so I don't ask,' said Jack.

'Maybe Zizi the Soothsayer knows who he is. She and Ms Parnell were close friends. I daresay they compared notes about their lovers. Women do, don't they?'

'Not as much as men, according to DC Fox. I'll get Gemma to pay her another visit.'

* * *

When Jack opened his front door that evening, a glorious aroma of steak and kidney pie wafted towards him. He breathed it in hungrily. His wife, Corrie Dawes, was the owner and head chef of Coriander's Cuisine, a popular and lucrative catering company. Carlene, her business partner, managed Chez Carlene, a bistro with a strong French influence, where Zizi and Allegra had planned to meet for the fateful lunch that never happened. Together, Corrie and Carlene ran Corrie's Kitchen, a fast-food takeaway —"good food at affordable prices". All three businesses were very successful, and at one time or another, most of the good citizens of Kings Richington and the surrounding villages availed themselves of their services. With this in mind, Jack frequently took advantage of Corrie's ear-to-the-ground knowledge of what was going on locally. Tonight was no exception.

'Hello, darling. You're late.' Corrie took the pie from the oven, where it was keeping warm. 'I'm guessing it's the Parnell–Roberts murders. How's it going?'

Jack kissed her. 'No obvious suspects. In fact, no suspects at all. I don't suppose you've heard anything on your culinary grapevine that might give us a lead?'

Corrie put a large portion of pie on his plate and added some vegetables. 'I hope you're not implying that I listen to gossip.'

'Perish the thought, my little pie-making person. It's just that you spend a lot of time mingling with the public and you're very observant.' He took a huge mouthful of pie and huffed and puffed a bit.

'I was going to warn you. The pie's very hot.' She poured them a glass of Merlot. 'I suppose you know that Allegra Parnell was what they euphemistically call a "player".'

'I thought that was only blokes,' said Jack.

'You'd better not let your DC Fox hear you say that. She'll report you to the *Women for Global Domination Police*.'

'There's no such thing. You just made that up.'

'Possibly. All the same, Ms Parnell definitely liked to explore her options where men were concerned. I put it down to the fact that she lost her mum when she was little. No role model. Then just recently, she lost her dad as well. I used to cater dinner parties for Grafton Parnell. He was a nice enough chap but I believe he tended to bend the rules a bit for his wealthy clients. Allegra was the same — not much in the way of a moral compass.'

'Sweetheart, she was a divorce lawyer. It was bound to have an effect, listening to people complaining about their cheating spouses every day.'

Corrie pursed her lips. 'A judgemental person might say she was the cause of a lot of the cheating.'

Jack's eyes widened. 'What? You mean she drummed up business by luring other women's husbands into adultery and causing them to want a divorce?'

'No. It sounds crude when you put it like that, and it's almost certainly unethical. But she did like to sample some of the goods.'

'I don't suppose you know whose goods she was sampling at the time she was murdered? Her office manager was positive she was having an affair with some hunk, but unlike her other conquests, she hadn't mentioned his name.'

Corrie put down her knife and fork. 'That's what I heard. The word on the street is that as well as being married, the man in question is in a profession where extramarital hanky-panky would have damaged his prospects — that's if his wife didn't do it first.'

'You mean like a cabinet minister or a bishop?'

'Good Lord, no. I doubt if that would shock anyone. But there's a growing army of disapproving wokes in this town who feel they have a moral obligation to object to anyone who appears to be having a good time. This is either because they are genuinely concerned about the decline in decency and increase in turpitude, and seek to restore the order of things, or because they're a bunch of disappointed, sexually deprived, self-opinionated whingers with nothing better to do. My money's on the latter. I'll keep my ear to the ground.'

He grinned. 'Do you think having your ear to the ground might be something of a handicap when it comes to getting me another slice of pie?'

* * *

Next morning, the team assembled in the incident room and added their respective contributions to the whiteboard. It was filling up with questions but was parlously short of answers. Jack stood in front of it. 'Despite the information we've all gathered, there are still some important gaps that need filling to move the investigation forward. As a priority, we need to find out who Allegra's boyfriend was. Unlike her previous affairs, she didn't broadcast his name. He may not have anything to do with the murders, but on the other hand, he could be a key player and he's certainly a person of interest. Any luck with TIE, Clive?'

''Fraid not, boss. I've tried all the usual avenues and even some of the more obscure ones, but Ms Parnell kept this guy very close to her chest.'

'Lucky bastard,' someone murmured, and there were subdued sniggers.

'I wonder why she didn't want anyone to know who he was?' asked Aled. 'Maybe he wasn't up to her usual high standards. She might have been embarrassed about having a relationship with a bit of rough.'

'In that case, he was probably a copper,' muttered a woman officer. It was greeted by howls of male protest.

'I still believe Zizi Starr might know who he is,' said Jack. 'Gemma, give her another tug. Tell her she isn't being disloyal as her friend's dead and it just might help us to catch her killer.'

'Sir, I found a backstory on Zizi Starr that might be relevant,' offered Clive. 'Her real name is Zoe Slack. She was taken to court a while back for supplying a psychoactive substance in her shop.'

'She was dealing drugs?' asked Jack.

'Not exactly, sir. It was a so-called "legal high". Her defence lawyer . . . guess who . . .'

'Allegra Parnell,' they chorused.

'Correct. She claimed Zizi believed it to be herbal tea and that she had no reason to suspect that it contained a banned substance when she had it imported from China, along with a variety of other teas. It has since been confirmed that a good deal of Chinese tea is contaminated with lead, arsenic and aluminium.'

'Sounds a reasonable defence,' said Jack. 'What happened?'

'The magistrate was having none of it. He said the "reck-lessness test" meant she couldn't escape liability by arguing that she was unaware the psychoactive substance was likely to be consumed. It was clearly labelled "tea" and sold as such. She got a hefty fine and six months' suspended.'

'That's a bit harsh for a first offence like that,' said Bugsy. 'Who was the magistrate?'

Clive looked at his screen. 'Felix Telford Barrington. He has a reputation for handing out disproportionate pun-ishments, especially to women. They call him "Butcher Barrington" down the courts.'

'Why is he allowed to get away with it?' Gemma sat forward in her chair.

'He might not, for much longer,' said Clive. 'There are plans afoot to have him removed on the grounds of mis-behaviour and a persistent failure to meet the standards of competence as prescribed by the Lord Chancellor.'

'Good. The sooner the better.' Gemma sat back again.

'Clive, did you dig up any more about Kirsty Jackson, the girl who disappeared two years ago, and Brian Roberts' connection?'

'Yes, boss. I delved into the MISPER investigation.'

'Delve away, son,' said Bugsy. 'You're full of useful stuff today.'

'The night she disappeared, she'd been to a dance at the community centre in Kings Richington. It's a kind of youth project run by a bloke called Roger Goodman, presumably to keep the kids off the streets.'

'I remember going to a youth club when I was a teenager. Never kept us off the streets,' recalled Bugsy. 'We used to hang about outside drinking cheap cider all evening to avoid going in.'

Clive continued. 'Kirsty's boyfriend, Josh Barker, had just passed his driving test so they went in his newly acquired, battered old Mini. They left the dance early because she said she had a music exam next day and it was very important to her future. She didn't want to be tired. In his statement, Josh said he drove her to the crossroads, where they parted company. She said she'd walk the rest of the way home, to save him having to drive down the muddy road to the farm and back again. He said it was well-rutted with half-buried rocks and the suspension on his Mini was a bit suspect. It was less than half a mile. He arrived home safely but she didn't. At midnight, her parents, Ted and Mary Jackson, called the police because she wasn't answering her phone. There was a very thorough search but there was no sign of her after she got out of the car. Mr and Mrs Jackson did a television appeal and the boy was pulled in for questioning several times as he was the last person to see her, but she was never found.'

Aled remembered his theory about Brian Roberts. 'Sir, what if Roberts got a bit too fond of her? She was his protégée and they spent a lot of time together practising. Maybe he lay in wait for her and when Josh had dropped her off, he tried it on. She rejected him and he killed her in a fit of passion.'

'What did he do with her body?' someone asked.

'Why would he be interested in a sixteen-year-old, when he was married to Allegra Parnell?' asked someone else.

Aled continued, undaunted. 'If some new facts had come to light and her parents suspected Roberts had killed their daughter, maybe he was the intended victim. Allegra Parnell may have been the collateral damage.'

'Ted Jackson's a farmer,' added Clive. 'He owns a shotgun, legal and licensed. I checked. But there was never any suspicion that Roberts killed Kirsty. He was home with Allegra all that night, checking the music for Kirsty's exam next day. Allegra had brought some casework home.'

'He could have nipped out, supposedly to the loo, then come back in later, maybe without her even noticing. They weren't a particularly close couple,' Aled persisted.

'He could hardly have killed the girl and disposed of her body in the time it takes someone to have a pee,' said Bugsy. 'Not unless he had a very dodgy prostate.'

Jack frowned. 'We don't have any evidence that Roberts killed Kirsty or that Jackson suspected he did. It was two years ago and I'm reluctant to reopen old wounds by questioning Jackson and asking to see his shotgun. We'll add him to the whiteboard, Aled, as a possible person of interest.'

CHAPTER FOUR

DC Gemma Fox pulled up outside The Galaxy Boutique and saw at once the sign that read, "Closed Until Further Notice". It appeared that Zizi had gone to her cousin in Truro after all, despite being advised against it. Now the Cornwall cops would probably be asked to speak to her. Gemma walked up to the shop window and peered inside, shielding her eyes.

'You looking for Zizi?' said a voice behind her.

'Yes.' Gemma turned around. 'Do you know where she's gone?'

The man pointed. 'I own the butcher's shop next door. She came to tell me she was going away for a while but didn't tell me where, because she didn't want anybody to know. Said she was lying low for a while. She asked me to keep an eye on the boutique — give her a call if I saw anyone hanging about. So far, I've only seen you.'

Gemma produced her warrant card.

The man blinked. 'Police. Is she in trouble?'

'Not as far as I know. I just wanted to have a word. How did she seem when she spoke to you?'

'Scared shitless, pardon my French. Dunno why, though. But she mentioned something about a bad accident that had happened to her best friend and she didn't want the same thing to happen to her. Then she got into that Disney car of hers and shot off.'

'Would you mind giving me the number that she wanted you to call, in the event of a prowler?'

'Yeah, I suppose it's OK, you being a police officer.' He pulled out his phone and Gemma copied the number into hers.

'Thank you very much.' Gemma gave him her card. 'Perhaps you'd give me a ring if you do see anyone hanging about.'

* * *

When she got back to the station, Gemma phoned the number the butcher had given her. It rang a couple of times, then Zizi answered.

'Hello, who is this?'

'It's Detective Constable Fox, Ms Starr. I need to speak to you.'

'Go away! I've told you everything I know. Leave me alone!'

The phone went dead. Gemma pressed redial but Zizi had turned hers off. No doubt Clive would have some unfathomable system of tracing her location using her phone's GPS but what Gemma really wanted to know was why Zizi was indeed "scared shitless", to use the butcher's description. She would report it to the inspector at the next briefing.

* * *

So far, the MIT had drawn a blank — several blanks. They had taken copious statements from Allegra's colleagues at the Parnell & Parnell law firm and from Brian's fellow teachers at Kings Richington Comprehensive. Jack would have liked a list of Allegra's divorce clients at the time of her death but without a warrant, that was never going to happen – not on Jane Shaw's watch.

Officers had trawled through the couple's circumstances and habits and Jack had studied Dr Hardacre's detailed post-mortem report and the material gathered by the SOCOs. Clive had reported nothing untoward in either Allegra Parnell's or Brian Roberts' financial transactions, apart from the fact that she was much better off than him. But they already knew that from Ms Shaw's character assassination. They had used the media to broadcast requests for anyone with information to come forward. Jack was always reluctant to do this, as it created a "crackpot tsunami" for Norman and his officers on the front desk. Despite all this, the fact remained that they still had two dead people, both murdered with a missing shotgun, but no obvious motive and not a clue who had done it. It was while they were brainstorming that the door burst open and Chief Superintendent Garwood strode in.

'Morning, sir.' Jack stood to one side so that Garwood could look at the whiteboard. 'I thought you'd taken the morning off to play golf.'

'I did but my partner didn't turn up. Most unreliable. Didn't even have the decency to let me know. How is this case progressing?'

Jack was tempted to say that it wasn't, more like standing still, or even going backwards, but it was never a good idea to sound negative in front of the old man. He stonewalled. 'Early days, sir, but we are investigating every angle.'

Garwood peered for some moments at all the information that was written and pinned to the board. The room went silent.

Finally, he spoke. 'It seems to me, Inspector, that you're only seeing what's under your nose, and most of that's distorted.'

Jack wondered whether Garwood meant the case or his nose, conceding that he was right on both counts.

The DCS continued. 'It's as though you're looking at the facts through a cracked mirror. Cast your web a bit wider, Dawes. Get on with it, man — the commander wants results.

The press is leaning on him.' He marched out, oblivious to the disrespectful gestures that followed him.

'Tell you what, guv,' said Bugsy. 'To me, this is all about logic. We start with all the scenarios we can think of, then eliminate the ones it couldn't possibly be. Otherwise, we have too many distractions. Once we clear those out, we can focus on what's left, and with the impossible eliminated, what's left are the only possible solutions, and one of them must be the truth.'

'Excuse me.' Gemma interrupted their deliberations. 'Now that the chief super has referenced the ramblings of Tennyson, and Sergeant Malone has channelled Sherlock Holmes, might I respectfully suggest that "the way to get started is to quit talking and begin doing".'

'Don't tell me, let me guess,' said Bugsy. 'Emmeline Pankhurst.'

Gemma laughed. 'No, Sarge — Walt Disney, actually. I've been looking at the website of the Richington Youth Project.'

'That's where Kirsty Jackson was at a dance the night she disappeared,' recalled Aled.

'That's right. It's funded by various community charities and run by Roger Goodman. I think we should pay him a visit.'

'Why?' asked Aled. 'Apart from Brian Roberts having been Kirsty's music teacher, what else is there to connect the youth project to his murder? We've already discounted any possibility that he was lying in wait for her when she walked home.'

'There was a newsletter on the youth project's website written by one of the young women — an aspiring journo,' replied Gemma. 'Let me read you a bit of it: "Tonight, we were lucky to have an astrology demonstration from our regular Galaxy Guru, Zizi Starr, who was rocking a nice line in funky earrings and a jazzy top".'

'So the Starr woman is involved with the club.' Bugsy was impressed. 'That's a connection we didn't know about. Could it be relevant?'

'Zizi isn't telling us everything she knows and she believes she's in danger. I've phoned her mobile a few times but she won't speak to me. Maybe this Roger Goodman knows something.' Gemma was clearly anxious to speak to him.

'OK, Gemma. You discovered the link, so get over there and see what you can find out. In the meantime, Clive has tracked the location of Zizi's mobile to an address in Truro. I'll get in touch with the Devon and Cornwall lads and get them to interview Zizi Starr about Allegra Parnell's boyfriend.'

* * *

The Richington Youth Project met in the community hall every Saturday night. The rest of the week, the venue housed various other events such as indoor bowling, tea dances, bingo night and a crochet circle. For members of the community looking for real, unbridled excitement, there was a "Monopoly Monday" and a "Soup & Sweet Supper" on Sundays. Roger Goodman was chairperson of the community hall committee, main keyholder, caretaker and general dogsbody. He also had keys to the gym next door, where he worked out regularly, together with a number of the youngsters. It was a very popular activity as boys and girls alike all sought to be "fit". Goodman had been county middleweight boxing champion in his prime and coached any of the young people who were keen to learn. He was in good condition, and looked much younger than his forty-five years.

When Gemma arrived, he was cleaning up after a dog-training session, ably assisted by a young man, whom Gemma assessed to be in his late teens or early twenties. She produced her warrant card.

'Mr Goodman? I'm Detective Constable Fox from Kings Richington MIT. I wonder if you could spare me a few minutes.'

Goodman jammed his mop in the bucket and nodded to the lad to take over. 'Certainly, officer. How can I help?'

Gemma thought she may have been mistaken — she was unusually sensitive to atmosphere — but he seemed suddenly cautious, almost guarded. She watched his face for a reaction to her questions. 'You will have seen news of the two people found dead from gunshot wounds in Richington Mallet?'

'Yes, indeed. Terrible business. But what has it to do with the youth project? I don't believe either of those poor people ever came here.'

'I see from your website that Zizi Starr did, though. Did you know she was best friends with Allegra Parnell, one of the deceased?'

'No, I didn't. Zizi comes here to hold astrology sessions. The young people are very fond of her. She speaks their language and they like her rather unconventional style. We haven't seen her since the horrific murders, which is hardly surprising under the circumstances. She must be very upset.'

Gemma chose her words carefully. 'It was Zizi who found the bodies. She's very scared, Mr Goodman. Do you know why that might be?'

His brow furrowed while he thought about it. 'No, I'm afraid I don't, apart from that being a normal human response to the bloody murder of her friend. Perhaps you should ask her.'

Gemma detected a slight hostility in his tone. 'We shall. She has left Kings Richington and we're trying to locate her current whereabouts.'

Goodman called across to the young man. 'Josh, this officer is asking about Zizi. The police are trying to find her. How did she seem the last time she was here?'

'Jumpy,' replied Josh. He looked straight at Gemma. 'The cops still haven't found my Kirsty so I don't much rate your chances of finding Zizi.'

Gemma looked at him. This was Kirsty Jackson's boyfriend. Two years ago, he would have been sixteen or seventeen, which would make him about nineteen now. 'The case is still open, Josh. We've never given up looking.'

He wasn't impressed. 'Huh! Back then, you lot tried to fit me up — make out I'd killed her. Kept on pulling me in and questioning me. Even her parents suspected me for a while. Why would I have harmed Kirsty? I loved her. We were going to get engaged when she was eighteen. Get married, have kids and run her parents' farm when they retired. Never happened, did it?'

Gemma felt sorry for him. It seemed he was still grieving for the future he had been looking forward to, even after two years. She asked, gently, 'What do you think happened to Kirsty?'

'S'obvious, innit? Some bastard killed her and did away with her body.' He walked away.

'Will that be all, Constable Fox?' Goodman's face was expressionless.

'For now, Mr Goodman. We may need to speak to you again.'

He watched Gemma go out to her car, climb in and drive away. Then he pulled out his phone and punched the speed dial number. 'The police were here but it's OK. They were just asking about Zizi Starr.'

* * *

Zizi was out of the shower and towelling her hair when the video doorbell of her cousin's house began playing 'Autumn' from Vivaldi's *Four Seasons*. As well as a number of other clever functions, it was set up to change concerto in line with the changing seasons. Not that Zizi would have appreciated it as she was more of a rap and hip-hop girl. Her cousin had explained that if anybody called, the smart system meant she could see, hear and speak to whoever was on the doorstep by using her phone, tablet or any other device near to hand.

Zizi was alone in the house apart from the baby that she had offered to look after while her cousin was shopping. She looked at the screen and saw two police officers on the doorstep — Police Constable Blake and Police Constable Davis from the Truro Station.

For heaven's sake, she raged silently. *How did they find me? Why don't they leave me alone?* She ignored them and ducked down out of sight behind the sofa.

They began walking around the house peering in windows. *They'll get fed up soon and go away*, she thought.

Then the baby woke up and began crying. He had powerful lungs and it was obvious the police had heard him. They pressed the bell again and banged on the door. Zizi didn't want them breaking in, believing there was a baby alone in the house, so she was forced to speak to them, but she had no intention of letting them in.

'Hello. What do you want? Stop banging — you've woken the baby.'

'We need to speak to Ms Zizi Starr.' PC Davis held her warrant card up to the camera. 'Is she there?'

'Yes, I'm Zizi Starr. What do you want?'

'We need to speak to you, miss. Can we come in?'

'No. I've just come out of the shower and I'm not decent and now I have to go and settle the baby. Unless you have a warrant, you're not coming in.'

The two officers conferred. They'd been told to question her about the identity of her deceased friend Allegra Parnell's boyfriend. There had been no mention of a warrant. They had no reason to suspect she had committed a crime apart from leaving the area after she'd been advised to stay. But that didn't justify arresting her and taking her down to the Devon & Cornwall nick.

PC Blake took over. 'We're acting on behalf of the Kings Richington Major Incident Team, Ms Starr. They want to know the name of Ms Allegra Parnell's boyfriend at the time of her murder and any other information that might be relevant.'

Zizi thought about it. Unlike all the others, Allegra hadn't wanted her affair with this particular guy made common knowledge, for some reason. But her friend was dead so what harm could it do now? More to the point, it couldn't make her own situation much riskier and maybe the cops would leave her alone. 'She didn't tell me his name but he was one of your lot.'

The two officers looked at each other, puzzled. 'Do you mean he was a police officer?' asked PC Davis.

'Yes. He was one of the two coppers who came to Allegra's house after I dialled 999. I recognized him because he once came to pick her up from my shop. She'd been round for drinks with me after work.'

'Can you describe him?' asked PC Blake.

'I'd guess he was mid-thirties, good-looking, muscular, probably works out — just Allegra's type. He and another officer were first to arrive after I called the police. They went inside then he ran back out and was sick on the doorstep. Now go away and leave me alone. I've nothing more to say without my solicitor.' Tears welled up in her eyes. 'Oh, I forgot. She's dead.'

CHAPTER FIVE

'Well, Constable Walker, what have you got to say for yourself?' Sergeant Parsloe was confronting Wayne Walker about his affair with Allegra Parnell. 'I trust you're not going to deny it. If necessary, I'll bring Ms Starr in and we'll carry out an identification, but she has already confirmed it was you from the photo we sent to her phone.'

Jack and Bugsy were present at the interview but thought it best left to Walker's senior officer. As far as they could see, Walker wasn't involved in the murders other than being first on the scene when the bodies were discovered. On the other hand, nothing could be taken for granted. They had precious few leads left and had reached the point where nothing could be discounted.

Walker was clearly still in shock but defiant. 'I've done nothing wrong, Sergeant.'

'Nothing wrong?' Parsloe was incensed. 'You've got a wife and two kiddies and you've been going over the side with a married woman.' Norman was one of a dying breed, who believed this kind of behaviour was reprehensible wherever it occurred, never mind in the police service. 'How can you stand there and tell me you've done nothing wrong?'

'It isn't a crime, Sergeant.'

Jack intervened. 'No, Constable Walker, adultery may be regarded as a sin by some but it isn't a crime. However, withholding evidence in a serious murder case most certainly is. You were first on the scene. You knew the murdered woman intimately and should have declared a conflict of interest and walked away.'

'Instead,' added Bugsy, 'you confused the investigation by leaving your DNA and fingerprints all over the house, presumably to disguise the fact that there were already plenty of them in the bedroom.'

'Whatever were you thinking, man?' asked Parsloe. 'You're a good copper. How did you come to be involved with Allegra Parnell?'

'She came to the station to represent one of her clients in a shoplifting charge. The woman had accidentally put a chicken in her bag without paying for it. She claimed she was going through a traumatic divorce and didn't know what she was doing. Allegra got her off, despite the magistrate being Butcher Barrington. He wanted to sentence her to six months inside. Allegra told him he was a bully and a misogynist and she intended to report him to the Lord Chancellor. He backed down. She was an amazing woman — beautiful, clever, funny, dangerous — I was in love with her.'

'Was she in love with you?' asked Jack.

Walker hesitated as though the recollections were painful. 'No, sir. I asked her to run away with me and she laughed. She said I was taking it too seriously and I needed to lighten up. I was becoming boring, like Brian.'

'How did that make you feel, son?' asked Bugsy. 'Were you angry?'

'To start with. But I just wanted to go on seeing her, so I went along with it, on her terms.'

'Do you own a shotgun, Constable Walker?' asked Jack.

'Yes, sir. We live out in the country, close to Richington Forest. There's a problem with rats getting into the house and the wife is scared of them so I keep them down. I wouldn't use poison because of my kids.' He suddenly realized the purpose of the question. 'You don't think I shot Allegra? I couldn't. I adored her.'

'Maybe it was just a rush of blood, son,' suggested Bugsy. 'You didn't mean to do it, but you weren't thinking clearly. You realized that you were just one in a succession of lovers and soon, she'd move on to the next one. You decided if you couldn't have her, nobody would—'

'No! No! It wasn't me!' Sobbing, Wayne Walker made for the door, where he was restrained by his erstwhile colleague, PC Johnson. Sergeant Parsloe gave him a nod and Johnson escorted him from the room.

'What do we think?' asked Jack.

'He wouldn't be the first bloke to commit murder over a woman,' said Bugsy. 'Love — Lust — Loathing — Loot. They're the Four Horsemen of the . . . er . . . Puckerlips — the main motives for murder. He could have felt the first three. Love because he thought he did, lust because he certainly did, and loathing when she made him feel a twerp. I doubt if loot came into it, although she wasn't short of a few bob. You only have to look at her house and car.'

'Do we know his whereabouts between seven and midnight on the night of the shootings?' asked Jack.

'He says he was at home with his wife and kids,' replied Parsloe.

'We need to check that out. And get Ballistics to test his shotgun.'

'You don't really think Walker was responsible for two murders, do you, Jack?' Parsloe was doubtful. 'He was a good lad before that witch got her claws into him.'

'To be honest, Norman, I don't know what I think, but we've reached the point where we need to check out everything, however unlikely.'

* * *

DI Dawes sent DC Fox to speak to Walker's wife. Tracy Walker was cooking the children's tea — fish fingers, chips and peas.

'Please come in, Constable. Excuse the mess but I'm under the cosh a bit at the moment.' She didn't explain why. 'I expect you're here about Allegra Parnell. What a terrible thing to have happened. And her poor husband, too.'

Gemma was on the back foot. She'd been told to tread carefully because as far as they knew, Mrs Walker wasn't aware of her husband's affair. 'What makes you think that?'

'Well, it was all over the news. I imagine the police will want to speak to everyone who had any contact with her.'

Gemma thought she seemed remarkably calm. 'What contact did you have with her, Mrs Walker?'

Tracy looked surprised. 'She was my solicitor, wasn't she? I thought you knew that. Isn't that why you're here?'

Gemma didn't answer that. 'May I ask why you needed a solicitor?'

'I'm divorcing Wayne, and she was the best in the business at getting what you're entitled to. You must have seen her on Twitter —@DivorceDiva? She was expensive but my parents were helping me. They never wanted me to marry Wayne in the first place. My dad doesn't trust the police — no offence.'

'Do you mind telling me why you want a divorce, Mrs Walker?'

'The bastard's having an affair. I don't know who with but I've found all the signs. A burner phone, perfume on his clothes, sexy new underpants and receipts for dinners at that posh bistro in town, Chez Carlene. No interest in me or the kids. Allegra said not to worry. Under the new law, we didn't need to know who the bitch was because we could still take him for everything he earned.' She sighed. 'I suppose I'll have to start all over again, now that she's gone.' She served up the children's tea and called them in from the garden.

Gemma looked at their faces while they ate, oblivious to the upheaval that was about to happen to them. The boy was wearing a football shirt and the girl was dressed as a unicorn fairy. They'd cope, decided Gemma. Having divorced parents was something of a status symbol nowadays. You got twice as many treats and presents and you could play one off against the other. In Gemma's view, the only certain way to avoid divorce was not to get married in the first place.

'One last question, Mrs Walker. Can you tell me where your husband was between seven and midnight on the night of the shootings?'

Tracy looked at the notes on the fridge calendar, where she had circled the fateful date. 'Well, I was at the cinema. It was the new version of *Death on the Nile*. The kids were having a sleepover at my mum's house. I couldn't tell you where Wayne was, he went out before I did. He was probably with his tart.' She thought for a bit, then the penny dropped. 'Why do you want to know? You can't think Wayne's a suspect in her murder because she was helping me with the divorce? That's ridiculous!'

* * *

'She was a piece of work, that Allegra Parnell,' declared Bugsy. Back in the incident room, Gemma was adding the new information to the whiteboard. 'She's acting for Tracy Walker in her divorce application when she's the other woman who's having it off with her husband. Priceless! You couldn't make it up.'

Jack remembered Corrie saying that Allegra might have been the cause of the irretrievable breakdown in some of the divorce cases she handled and that she liked to 'sample the goods'. He'd been doubtful at the time, but here was an actual example. He wondered how the Law Society would have looked upon it if they'd found out, even though adultery was no longer needed as grounds for divorce.

'Uniform have impounded PC Walker's shotgun, sir, and Ballistics are testing it,' reported Clive. 'Incidentally, I checked the shotgun licensing authority. It seems Mrs Walker has a licence as well. She shoots clays.'

'Does she indeed? And she doesn't have an alibi for that night, either, apart from Hercule Poirot.'

'Well, I reckon we've pretty much cracked it,' claimed Aled. 'When the Ballistics report comes back, it'll show that it was the Walkers' gun that killed Allegra and poor old Brian.'

'Serves him right,' said Bugsy. 'He should have been up the pub playing darts and getting lashed instead of sitting at home playing the piano.'

'Or even up the pub, playing the piano,' added Mitch.

'My guess,' continued Aled, undeterred, 'is that the killer was either PC Walker, annoyed because Allegra had given him the elbow, or Mrs Walker because somehow she'd found out that Allegra was hubby's bit on the side and she'd been double-crossed. Either way, we've got our killer banged to rights.'

'Aled, son, don't let anyone ever tell you your thought processes are too complex,' said Bugsy.

'You can take the mickey, Sarge, but I bet I'm right.'

'Sir?' Clive called out from his desk surrounded by multiple IT devices that only he understood. 'The email with the Ballistics report has just come in. The Walkers' shotgun was definitely *not* the one used to kill Allegra Parnell and Brian Roberts.'

'Bugger!' cursed Aled. 'Back to square one.'

* * *

When Jack got home, Corrie and her business partner, Carlene, were sitting at the dining table drinking a glass of dry white wine and deciding on a menu for an important dinner party they'd been hired to cater. Until recently, Carlene had been Corrie's deputy. She was much loved by both Corrie and Jack, who had given her a home from the halfway house she'd ended up in after being brought up in care. Over the years, Corrie had trained her, and Chez Carlene, the bistro that she ran with her French boyfriend, Antoine, had won a Michelin star, proof of her undoubted talents and hard work. It was time, Corrie had decided, to make her a partner in the business. She looked up as Jack came in. 'Hello, darling. Good day?'

Jack sank down into an armchair. 'No, it's been a bloody awful day, thanks for asking.'

'What's the matter, Inspector Jack?' Carlene poured him a glass of wine. She'd called him that, or Mr Jack, from the time she'd come to live with them and now couldn't imagine calling him anything else. It was a term of respect and affection, in much the same way that she called Corrie Mrs D.

'It's the shotgun shootings — only I'm not supposed to talk about it, because we still haven't caught who did it.'

'It wasn't PC Walker or his wife, then?' asked Corrie, without looking up from the list of starters.

'How did you know they were suspects?' Jack was shocked. 'We've only just ruled them out ourselves.'

'News travels fast,' she replied.

'We had Tracy Walker's mum in Corrie's Kitchen today. She was buying pizza for the children's tea,' said Carlene. 'Tracy's left him and taken the kids to live with her parents until she can find another solicitor to take on her divorce application. Then she's going to take him for every penny he's got, including the house.'

'No wonder Allegra didn't want to say who her current boyfriend was,' said Corrie. 'She was screwing Wayne at the same time as acting for his wife in a divorce case. Although, in reality, the reasons a marriage has irretrievably broken down rarely make a difference to the financial settlement, so I guess she thought it didn't matter.'

'She had some nerve, I'll say that for her,' conceded Carlene. 'I wonder if she thought she could get away with Tracy not knowing before she finalized her divorce paperwork?'

Corrie shrugged. 'I expect she'd have moved on to someone else by then. She never kept one for very long.'

Jack was shocked. 'Allegra *is* dead, you know. You two make her sound like some irresponsible person who keeps adopting rescue dogs, getting fed up with them and taking them back again.'

'Well, when you come right down to it,' said Carlene, 'that's pretty much what she was doing. Only this time, someone put a stop to her.'

'I don't suppose your rumour mill has any insight into who that was?' asked Jack. 'Because we well-meaning amateurs down at the nick don't have much to go on at the moment.'

Corrie screwed up her face. 'No, but do you want us to tell you what we think?'

'Do I have a choice?'

'Not really. We don't think she was killed because she was promiscuous, unethical and a functioning sociopath – although she was all of those things. We think it was because of something she'd found out.'

'Like what?'

'Dunno. We're still working on that one. We'll let you know when we come up with something. But if I were you, I'd get a warrant and go through Allegra's caseload. Something tells me there'll be a few clues in there. In the meantime, Carlene has cooked you some supper. She's practising a new dish that she wants to put on the menu at the bistro.'

Jack perked up. 'What is it, Carlene?'

'Lamb's sweetbreads poached in squid ink with a kale and spinach salad.' She gave Corrie a conspiratorial glance.

'Lovely,' muttered Jack, wondering if he could sneak out to the pub for steak and chips. But he could never disappoint Carlene — the daughter he'd never had, but who he'd come to love as if she were. If she'd cooked it for him, then he'd eat it, no matter how disgusting it tasted.

She went into the kitchen and returned with a cloche-covered plate. She whipped off the dome and put the steaming plate of food on the dining table in front of him. 'There you go, Inspector Jack. Get your choppers round that. Ribeye steak with scalloped potatoes, haricots verts à la Dijonnaise and a roasted onion salad with a walnut salsa.'

'Wonderful!' Suddenly, all the trials and frustrations of the day melted away, and Jack smiled to himself. He wondered whether, when Carlene served steak to her upmarket, Michelin-starstruck diners at the bistro, she told them to 'get their choppers round it'.

CHAPTER SIX

The team continued to work on anything that might possibly lead to a breakthrough. Nothing did. Remembering Corrie's advice, which made sense, Jack went down the corridor to Chief Superintendent Garwood's office and knocked.

Garwood took the glass of single malt he'd just poured and put it in his drawer. He grabbed a bundle of files from the top of the cupboard behind him and piled them up in his in-tray, so it appeared to be overflowing. 'Come,' he called out.

Jack got straight to the point. 'Sir, I need a search warrant. I know I could apply to the court myself, but it will carry more weight coming from you. In the past, it's taken anything up to three weeks to come through, by which time any evidence has been lost or removed.'

'I assume this is to do with the shotgun killings?'

'Yes, sir. I need access to Allegra Parnell's caseload. I believe one of her clients may have been involved — either directly or indirectly.'

'What exactly are you hoping to find, Inspector?'

'I don't know until I look, sir. Her practice was a little, shall I say, unconventional. She had her own methods that suited her lifestyle.'

Garwood grunted acknowledgement. 'My wife may have mentioned something of the sort. Ms Parnell did lay herself open to gossip. What about the other deceased — Brian Roberts?'

'We found nothing to indicate that anybody would want him dead. I'm inclined to believe that the only reason he was killed was because he witnessed his wife being shot. The team concluded that if he'd been out that night, he'd probably still be alive.'

'Poor devil. Bad luck.' This was as close as Garwood came to an expression of sympathy. He pressed the button on his intercom.

Nancy, his recently acquired personal assistant responded, brightly, 'Yes sir?

'Nancy, get me Felix Barrington. Not his home number. He's a magistrate, he'll be somewhere in the courts.' He returned to Jack. 'Barrington's my golf partner. I may be able to speed things up. This murder case is top priority. Sir Barnaby is having to answer some awkward questions from the press, who want to know why the police haven't arrested anyone yet.' Emotive as ever, the editor of the *Richington Echo* had emblazoned his front page with — *Are we all to be murdered in our beds before the police emerge from their torpor and catch the Shotgun Killer?*

Jack took this to mean that the commander was, in turn, leaning on Garwood, whose interpretation of the chain of command was that 'shit rolls downhill'.

Garwood's intercom buzzed. 'Sir, I've tried the magistrates' court and a Mr Percy Ponsonby, the clerk to the justices, says Mr Barrington hasn't been in since last week. So I telephoned his home and his wife said that he's away on business and she doesn't know when he'll be back.'

Garwood harrumphed. 'Get me another magistrate. Tell them I need a search warrant urgently.' *That explains why Felix didn't turn up for our golf match*, thought Garwood. *If he knew he was going to be away, why didn't the blasted man let me know? Damned rude, not to say inconvenient. But what can you expect from a man who once made a living selling waistcoats?*

* * *

Before Jack and the team had time to deploy the warrant, something more pressing occurred. The phone rang in the incident room. It was Sergeant Parsloe on the front desk. As Jack had predicted, their lines had been swamped by crackpots claiming the 'shotgun killer' was their estranged spouse, trying to prevent the Divorce Diva from taking them to the cleaners. This latest call, however, was something quite different.

Bugsy answered. 'Norman, don't tell me — Wyatt Earp's been at it again and you've got another gunfight at your OK Corral.'

'No, Bugsy, but I think you and Jack need to know about this. I've had a call from a man and his wife. They're mycophiles and apparently they like to pursue their hobby in Richington Forest. They're in there now.'

'Well, tell them to put their clothes back on and pack it in immediately — it's a disgusting habit. Fancy boasting about it to the police. They want locking up.'

'Do you know what mycology is, Bugsy?'

'Not a clue, Norman.'

'It's the study of fungi.'

'What? You mean they're picking mushrooms in the nude? Don't they know you can buy 'em in the supermarket? They'd have to put their clothes on first, though.'

Norman sighed. 'Bugsy, this is important. They were calling to report that they've found a man hanging from a tree in the Kings Copse. I told them to stay there and not to touch anything. I've sent my lads out to secure the scene and Dr Hardacre's on her way. It looks like a suicide but you can never be sure until the medics have had a poke about. I thought Jack would want to be informed, because Constable

Johnson reported the presence of a shotgun lying among the dead leaves at the foot of the tree. It's got what looks like dried blood on it. Obviously, he didn't touch it.'

'Blimey! OK Norman. We're on our way.'

* * *

Richington Forest had long been the subject of apocryphal tales of evil. There had been rumours of ogres, demons and screams of terror coming from among the trees, especially at night. The concept of a "Beast of Richington Forest" still endured, with sightings reported at regular intervals, mostly by drunks on their way home from the Richington Arms. Over the years, folklore had morphed into urban myth and now many citizens of a nervous disposition avoided going there, despite it offering a useful shortcut from one side of town to the other.

The clearing in the heart of the forest was relatively welcoming. On summer days, rays of sunlight filtered through the trees creating a dappled green carpet, a favourite venue for picnics and nature lovers. The Kings Copse, however, was dark, dank and fetid all year round. It formed a secluded corner of the forest where the sunlight never penetrated, hence the dead and decaying matter, old tree stumps and rotting leaf litter. This environment made it ideal for fungal species of all kinds.

By the time Jack and Bugsy arrived, uniformed officers had secured the scene and removed some of the razor wire fence that had effectively cut off Kings Copse from the rest of the forest. They had also taken down signs saying *Keep Out* and *Trespassers Will Be Prosecuted*. There was even one threatening that *Intruders Will Be Shot*.

Jack looked up at the body of a man hanging from the branch of an oak tree, his head lolling onto his chest. It was deadly still; no wind stirred among the broad branches. The air was thick, almost hard to breathe, and there was an unpleasant odour of rotting flesh. Jack's overriding thought concerned the psychology of suicide. What possible circumstance could be so overwhelming and desperate to drive a human being to such a terrible, hopeless end? His reflections were cut short by the arrival of Dr Hardacre, prompt and businesslike as always.

'Well, Inspector, you've scored your hat trick — that's three bodies now. Although I didn't expect to see you here. I didn't think the murder squad turned out for suicides.'

'Are we certain this bloke committed suicide, Doc?' asked Malone.

'Not yet, Sergeant. I'll let you know after I've taken him apart, but on the face of it, it seems more than likely, wouldn't you say?'

Jack crouched down and peered at the double-barrelled shotgun lying among the rotting vegetation, immediately below the body and next to an empty whiskey bottle. It had two spent cartridges sticking out of the chamber and was covered in dried blood. 'Can you ask SOCOs to do a complete sweep of this weapon including Ballistics tests, please?'

'Of course.' She called to the coppers. 'OK, cut him down now, please, and be careful, he looks a bit fragile. I don't want him already in pieces before I get him on the slab. And don't disturb the rope around his neck. I want it intact.'

'How long has he been up there, Doc?' asked Bugsy.

'Like I said, it's impossible to tell for certain until after the post-mortem.'

She examined the body briefly after they'd lowered him down. 'At a guess, I'd say less than a week, but possibly longer.'

Bugsy counted on his fingers. 'Wouldn't that make it around the time that the shotgun killings took place, guv?'

'Let's not jump to conclusions,' said Jack. 'We'll know more after Forensics have had time to do the tests.'

Dr Hardacre beckoned to the mortuary attendants. 'Right, you can put him in the meat-wagon now.'

After she'd gone, Jack looked around. 'Who found the body?'

'A couple of mycologists, according to Norman,' said Bugsy. 'Makes a change from joggers and dog walkers, I suppose.' He sniffed. 'Although I doubt whether ordinary folk would want to come into this copse — it's 'orrible. And what's with the razor wire and notices?' Isn't it public property, like the forest?'

'Dunno. We'll get Clive to look into it. Determining ownership of land, especially woodland, can be complicated.'

Jack and Bugsy made their way across the dank copse to where a middle-aged couple were waiting patiently by a police car.

'I'm Detective Sergeant Malone and this is Detective Inspector Dawes. And you are—?'

'Mr and Mrs Marlow.' The man looked a little overawed.

'Please — John and Jean,' insisted Mrs Marlow.

'How did you come to find the . . . er . . . deceased?' asked Jack.

'We were looking for the octopus stinkhorn,' said Jean. 'It hatches from a type of egg and has red tentacles, splayed out like a starfish.'

'Also called Devil's Fingers,' added her husband. 'It's fairly rare in the UK but this dark, moist copse is ideal. Fungi thrives off rotten wood and in damp conditions. The environment needs to be as dark as possible for them to spawn.'

'The tentacles can be up to seven centimetres long and they're covered in a dark green slime that attracts insects to distribute the spores.' Jean was getting into her stride. 'They smell like rotting flesh, which is what attracts the flies.'

Nice, thought Bugsy. 'Yes, but why were you looking for it here?'

'Because a member of our club — Friends of the Fungus — reckoned he'd spotted one in the Kings Copse but he couldn't get in there to take photographs because he was threatened by a man with a gun. Got told to bugger off in no uncertain terms. Well, I wasn't having that! There's a public footpath that goes right through here and we've every right to use it. So we came along with our wire cutters and in we went.' Jean brandished them. 'Mind you, we hadn't reckoned on finding him strung up to that tree.' She pointed up to the branch of the oak. 'Not that he didn't deserve it, miserable old sod.'

'Jean,' admonished her husband. 'It's bad luck to speak ill of the dead. Mind you, I never had him down as one for suicide. He was too full of himself for that.'

Jack and Bugsy exchanged glances. 'Do you know who he is?'

'Oh yes,' said Jean. 'He is — he *was* — Felix Barrington, the magistrate. Self-styled squire, lord of the manor and jumped-up pain in the arse.'

'Very feudal,' agreed her husband. 'The shotgun that was lying down there on the ground, before your people in overalls took it away—' he pointed under the tree — 'It was his, the same one he used to take potshots at unfortunate animals and to threaten people when they tried to get into his precious copse.'

'I wonder why he didn't just shoot himself?' pondered Jean. 'Strange bringing a shotgun to commit suicide then deciding to hang yourself instead. Less messy, though.'

'Maybe his arms weren't long enough,' suggested John. 'He was a small man — in lots of ways.'

'Did you find it? The stinky octopus thing?' asked Bugsy.

'No,' said Jean. 'We were rather distracted by the body. But once the police are done here, we'll be back.'

'We'll have a proper look,' confirmed her husband.

'Well, if you've finished with us, we'll be off home,' declared Jean. 'There's a club meeting tonight. We'll have plenty to report, won't we, dear?'

'Thank you,' said Jack. 'Just leave your contact details with that officer over there, if you wouldn't mind.'

They hurried off, leaving Jack and Bugsy bemused. 'What did you make of that, guv?'

'Fascinating. Not only did we get our corpse identified but we had a natural history lesson on the octopus stinkhorn.'

Bugsy's stomach was rumbling. He looked at his watch. 'Nothing more for us here, then. No obvious evidence of foul play. It'll be one for Uniform and the coroner to sort out.'

Jack was pensive. Like Gemma, he was sensitive to atmosphere and he didn't like what he was feeling in this creepy copse. Even though the body had been removed, there remained a heavy, sinister air of dread and disaster – as if the hanging wasn't the only bad thing to have happened here and there was more wickedness to come.

Pull yourself together, Dawes, he berated himself. *You're turning into Zizi Starr with your gloomy predictions. You'll be telling fortunes next. It's facts that count.*

He indicated to Bugsy that they should leave. 'Let's wait and see what Big Ron turns up.'

CHAPTER SEVEN

Uniform did the death call. Two constables visited Mrs Mallory Barrington the same day that Felix's body was found. They rang the bell of the impressive, ivy-covered house and after a few moments, a smartly dressed woman in her forties opened the door. They could hear dogs barking inside. The woman was wearing navy trousers, a floral blouse and a cashmere cardigan, with her blonde hair tied up in a neat bun. She looked from one officer to the other, a wary expression on her face. 'Yes? Can I help?'

They identified themselves, then the female officer said, 'Mrs Barrington? I'm afraid we have some bad news. May we come in, please?'

She shook her head. 'I'd rather you didn't. Strangers upset my dogs. Please just tell me what you've come to say.'

'It's your husband, Mr Felix Telford Barrington. I'm afraid he's been found dead in the Kings Copse. We're very sorry for your loss.'

* * *

Afterwards, the constables reported to Sergeant Parsloe that Mrs Barrington had been upset but didn't seem overly shocked. He repeated the information to Dawes.

'It was a bit odd, Jack,' said Norman. 'She thanked my officers for coming to tell her, but she didn't ask about the manner of Barrington's death, which is most unusual. Most bereaved relatives want to know how their loved one died, whether they suffered — all the details, especially if there's somebody they can sue or if it affects the life insurance. My officers simply told her that her husband's body had been found earlier that day in the Kings Copse and that seemed to be enough for her. They didn't press any distressing details on her, like he'd been found hanging from a tree, just that he was dead. She hadn't invited them in so they didn't want her passing out on the doorstep. She asked when she could arrange the funeral and they told her that would be down to the coroner. She didn't ask to see her husband but they told her she'd be needed to identify the body. Then they left.'

'Grief takes people in different ways,' observed Jack. 'Some people cope better by knowing less.'

'How long did Doc Hardacre say Barrington had been dead?' asked Clive.

'We haven't had the post-mortem report yet but she reckoned about a week,' said Bugsy. 'Why?'

'I checked the MISPER cases,' replied Clive, 'but Mrs Barrington never reported her husband missing. I wonder why.'

'When he didn't turn up for his golf match with the old man, she said he was away on business,' said Bugsy.

'Yeah, but I checked with Mr Ponsonby, the clerk to the justices, and he said Barrington was supposed to be in court all last week but simply hadn't turned up,' added Aled. 'He hadn't let anyone know and they'd had to get a replacement magistrate at short notice. It was all very inconvenient, Mr Ponsonby said, and not like Mr Barrington at all.'

'That is odd, Aled,' agreed Jack. 'On the other hand, if you were planning to do away with yourself, you wouldn't announce it first, in case people tried to stop you.'

'No, but you might just tell them you were taking a few days off instead of leaving them in the lurch. He was meant to be a responsible official.'

'I'm getting the feeling that you don't think it was a straightforward suicide, Aled. Why is that?'

'Dunno, boss. Nothing that would stand up in court, just a gut feeling. Mr and Mrs Marlow described him as—' he looked at what Bugsy had written at the time — '"too full of himself for suicide, a self-styled squire, lord of the manor and a jumped-up pain in the arse". He obviously believed himself to be an important man and demanded that everybody else thought the same.'

'He was an arrogant misogynist with a reputation for handing out disproportionate punishments, especially to women. They called him "Butcher Barrington" down at the magistrates' courts,' Gemma reminded them. 'That doesn't sound like a man who'd do everyone a favour and top himself.'

'On the other hand,' said Clive, 'there were efforts in place to get him struck off for misbehaviour and failure to meet proper standards. His ego can't have been very happy about that.'

'He'd have just found a way to wriggle out of it,' said Gemma. 'He wouldn't have hanged himself.'

'We're all ignoring an important question,' said Mitch. 'Why were the deceased and his shotgun covered in blood?'

'And whose blood was it?' asked Aled.

'It could have been animal blood,' said Jack. 'The Marlows said he was fond of taking potshots at unfortunate wildlife. Or maybe he'd had a few tentative attempts at slashing his wrists, although I don't believe SOCOs found a knife at the scene. Anyway, until we hear different from Dr Hardacre, we don't have anything specific to indicate that MIT should get involved. As far as we can tell, it was a suicide. We need to focus on the shotgun killings.' But he still had that uncomfortable doubt niggling away at the back of his mind.

* * *

'I doubt there'll be many people at Barrington's funeral,' remarked Corrie. 'The man was a crook, a bully and a pest.'

Jack was watching the rugby on TV and only half-listening. 'And on what personal experience do you base that purely unbiased indictment, sweetheart?'

'He tried to have Corrie's Kitchen closed down, the bastard.'

Jack suddenly leaped in the air and roared.

'Yes, that was my reaction, too,' declared Corrie, unaware that Jack's team had just scored a try. 'He said it was too close to Richington Comprehensive and that we were tempting the students to eat unhealthy junk food.'

'That's total bollocks!' declared Jack. 'The bloke needs his eyes tested.' The referee had disallowed the try.

'Absolutely! We give them pasta, wraps, salads, berries — all healthy stuff and most of them prefer it. We present it in a way that's tasty and appetizing. No hungry kid wants a few lettuce leaves, a raw carrot and a couple of grapes for their lunch, do they?'

Jack was still protesting over the disallowed try and he suspected partiality by the referee. 'Why do you suppose he did that? I reckon he had an ulterior motive.'

'He most certainly did,' agreed Corrie. 'One of Barrington's cronies wanted to start up a burger van outside the school. Richington Council's rules state that takeaways yet to receive planning permission are prevented from opening close to one another, so Barrington wanted to close us down. Bloody cheek! He didn't succeed though. And another thing — he was a sex pest. He used to kerb crawl in Kings Richington's red-light district.'

The match had paused for half-time so Jack heard the last bit. 'Did he really? No wonder his eyesight's bad. They say too much sex can affect your—'

'Well, I suppose it doesn't really matter now,' interrupted Corrie.

'Yes, it does. There's the second half to go, yet, and if the ref can't see what's right in front of him—'

'Jack, you're impossible! You haven't been listening to a word I've said, have you?'

'Erm . . . I heard something about food. Any chance of a snack before the second half, my little pasta person?'

Corrie put a plate of sandwiches and a bottle of beer in front of him. 'It's his wife I feel sorry for. Imagine two coppers coming and telling you your husband has hanged himself.'

'I don't believe they did tell her that, just that he was dead,' said Jack.

She ignored him and carried on. 'Thank goodness they didn't have any children. Mind you, she might have been glad. He was an awful man. If he'd been my husband, I shouldn't have waited for him to hang himself, I'd have choked the life out of him myself.'

'Don't you start,' complained Jack. 'I've got a team of detectives who are imagining all sorts of grisly scenarios and making up their own explanations. I've told them, unless we get any information to the contrary, it's suicide and it doesn't concern MIT.'

* * *

Next morning, Jack was even more convinced that he was right. The door of the incident room opened and Dr Hardacre poked her head round. In the modern world of pathology, it was becoming increasingly popular for post-mortems to be transmitted virtually, by way of forensic imaging. Some experts thought it improved clinical diagnosis of the immediate cause of death but not all pathologists were in favour. Dr Hardacre was one of these. 'I thought I'd bring you the post-mortem report myself, Inspector, as I suspect you'll have some questions.'

'That's good of you, Doctor. I know how busy you are.' Jack pulled up a chair for her and the team gathered round.

She opened a file. 'Felix Barrington had been dead around five to seven days when he was found. The exact timing is unclear due to the damp, humid environment. Cause of death was the compression of anatomical neck structures leading to asphyxia and neuronal death. Fatal strangling typically occurs in cases of violence and accidents and is one of the two main ways that hanging causes death, alongside breaking of the victim's neck.'

'So did he hang himself, Doc?' asked Bugsy.

'Maybe — maybe not. He still had traces of gunshot residue on his hands and some ante-mortem bruising to the chest, but that could have been sustained while climbing the tree. He also had a couple of dog bites, one on his arm and another on his leg. Quite fresh, about a week old, I'd say — you don't heal much after you're dead. But what I can tell you for certain is that the blood and bits of brain on his clothes and on the shotgun are a match for that of Allegra Parnell and Brian Roberts, and Ballistics' tests have proved it was the gun that was used to kill them. The only fingerprints, including the ones in the blood, belong to Barrington.'

'So that's the connection to our shotgun murders, sir,' concluded Aled with a degree of triumph. 'Barrington shot the two victims, drove back to the Kings Copse and hanged himself out of remorse.'

Gemma snorted. 'I don't believe that man would have known remorse if it had slapped him in his sneery face. Men like him need to be taught a lesson — that actions have consequences.'

'Right, Doc, so that's part of our mystery solved,' said Bugsy. 'We know who carried out the shootings — what we don't know is why. You don't kill two people just because they spilled your beer down the pub or cut you up at a roundabout. I doubt even Barrington was that deranged.'

'Precisely, Sergeant, but as I have pointed out on many occasions, I do the "how" and "when" — the "why" is your job.'

'Anything significant in the tox report, Doctor?' Jack wondered whether Barrington could have been on some kind of medication that had induced psychotic episodes.

She shook her head. 'Contrary to what television police dramas would have you believe, drug levels can rise, fall or even disappear entirely after death, potentially leading to incorrect conclusions about murder, suicide or overdose. Similarly, blood alcohol tests after death aren't reliable due to post-mortem fermentation, especially when the subject has been dead as long as Barrington. But judging by the empty whiskey bottle and the smell lingering in his clothes, he had probably drunk enough to render him unsteady at the very least. I'm surprised he had enough cognitive and physical ability to climb a tree, put a noose around his neck and jump. It's hardly surprising he bruised his chest in the process. Incidentally, the knot in the rope was tied some time ago.'

'You mean he'd been planning this for a while?' Jack was puzzled.

'Possibly. What I found was that the indentations on the rope made by the knot had been there for a long time — maybe even years. I doubt if anyone would plan their suicide that far ahead.'

'What sort of bloke carries a hangman's noose around for years?' Bugsy wondered.

'A magistrate with sick fantasies of hanging women for driving offences or shoplifting?' Gemma was scathing. 'He probably got off on it.'

Dr Hardacre stood up to go. 'One last detail you might wish to ponder, Inspector. His hyoid bone was fractured.'

'Wouldn't you expect that with a hanging, Doc?' asked Bugsy.

'Yes. Hyoid fractures in victims of strangulation and hanging are well defined, but it's more common in strangling than hanging. Fractures occur in around half of strangulations but only a third of hangings. Scientific experts insist that fractures of the hyoid bone are almost always associated with manual strangulation. Make of that what you will. I must go. I have customers dying to meet me.' She stomped out.

'Where do we go from here, sir?' asked Aled.

Jack frowned. He was unsure himself. 'On the face of it, we have two murders committed by a man we can't charge because he's hanged himself — if not from remorse, then to avoid a life sentence in a prison where some of the inmates might remember him – and not fondly.'

'It's well documented that suicide often follows a murder,' decreed Aled.

'So you said when you were trying to convince us that Brian Roberts shot Allegra, then himself,' said Gemma. She turned to Jack. 'Sir, I've been looking through Dr Hardacre's report. She found tiny fragments of a rare fungus, *Clathrus archeri*, in the hair on the back of Barrington's head.'

'It's octopus stinkhorn,' announced Clive, tapping away. 'It has red tentacles splayed out like a starfish, and they're covered in a dark green slime that—'

'Yes, we know what stinky octopuses are, son,' Bugsy announced. 'We had a lecture from the Marlows. They spawn on the ground in dark, damp mulch and eat rotten wood — not the Marlows, the stinky octopuses. The question is, how did it get in Barrington's hair? What was it doing up a tree?'

'Dr Hardacre said Barrington was probably very drunk before he died. Maybe he lay down and rested for a while, plucking up the courage to do it,' suggested Aled.

'Then he leaped to his feet, monkeyed up the tree, secured the rope, shouted "banzai" and jumped. Aled, son, he was middle-aged, unfit and plastered. If he'd decided he needed a lie down, he'd probably have dozed off and forgotten about the whole thing. It doesn't sound very likely, does it?'

'No, Sarge.' Aled had run out of ideas, which Jack thought was a pity because occasionally, he came up with a good one.

'Sir?' Mitch was dealing with the emails that were coming in. 'The coroner has raised concerns. She wants an antecedent report.'

'Right, so that's our next move,' instructed Jack. He wasn't surprised. There were too many loose ends and unknowns surrounding these cases. 'We put together a file of paper evidence based on four questions: Who died? When did they die? Where did they die? And, most importantly, how did they die? It isn't the coroner's role to attribute blame or put people on trial. That's our job and the CPS's, after we get the answers to the four questions.'

'What do you want us to do, sir?' asked Gemma.

'Bugsy and I will visit Mallory Barrington. We need a statement from her about the deceased's background and any relevant information about his health, physical and mental. If she has concerns about any of the circumstances surrounding Felix Barrington's death, she can raise them with us. We need to include Dr Hardacre's post-mortem report and any additional reports from the uniform officers — that means Norman's lads, especially Constable Wayne Walker and his wife. Also, eyewitnesses, even after the event, like the Marlows, and any other people we feel appropriate.'

'That means we go over a lot of information that we've already covered, only in more depth and now with an additional focus,' confirmed Bugsy.

'Of course, it will mean doing the same with the shotgun murders. These cases are closely linked so we have to treat them with equal importance,' added Jack. 'Keep in mind, we know Barrington shot Allegra Parnell and Brian Roberts, but we don't know why. We need to find the motive.'

'Where do we start, boss?'

'Gemma, I want you to speak to Zizi Starr again and try the bloke from the Richington Youth Project. You said at the time Goodman seemed a bit cagey. Lean on him. He might know something. Bugsy, go to Richington Comprehensive and ask more questions about Brian Roberts. He's the archetypal invisible man. He must have a few skeletons in his closet. Mitch, we now have a warrant to look through Allegra Parnell's divorce files. I'm sure there's a clue there somewhere. We have to find it. I realize this seems like double-handling, but we may find we get different answers to the same questions now that Barrington's dead. Right, people. Let's do it.'

CHAPTER EIGHT

Mallory Barrington was in her dead husband's dressing room, dragging his clothes from the wardrobe and stuffing them into black refuse sacks for the charity she supported. She'd been putting it off, reluctant to touch his things, but now that they'd found his body, it felt cathartic rather than distasteful. He had been a small man and had liked to dress precisely — to the point that he often looked ridiculous, in her view.

His decadent designer dressing gown was still lying on his bed. Felix had splashed out almost two thousand pounds on it, from a famous fashion house, saying he enjoyed the sensuous feel of real silk against his skin. Of course, it had been much too long for him, almost tripping him up. She smiled grimly to herself, remembering how he had strutted about the garden in it, pretending he was landed gentry, which he most certainly was not. She snatched it up and rammed it in the sack, along with all his other pretentious outfits.

Felix. That name was a joke, if ever there was one, thought Mallory. It meant "happy, fortunate" — the name of at least three popes, dozens of saints and the choice of hopeful parents everywhere wanting to bring their baby son good luck. Her own name — Mallory — was French in origin and meant "ill-omened". Well, wasn't that the truth? But not any longer.

The doorbell rang and she abandoned her task to go down and answer it. She'd had so many kind well-wishers bringing her flowers and sympathy. She liked to think she hadn't made the misery of her married life public, starting even from their honeymoon in Brightsea, which Felix had insisted on cutting short – regarding it an unnecessary waste of time and money. But people weren't blinkered. They could see for themselves.

Two men stood on the doorstep, holding out warrant cards. 'Mrs Barrington? Good morning. I'm Detective Sergeant Malone and this is Detective Inspector Dawes. We're from Kings Richington MIT.'

'Sorry to disturb you, madam,' said Jack. 'I wonder if we might have a few words.'

She looked a little nervous — most people did when confronted by plain-clothes police — but she was perfectly calm. 'Yes, of course. Please come in.'

They went through into an immaculate drawing room, fragrant from the many vases of flowers. The furnishings were luxurious, if not opulent, and the paintings on the walls were genuine. Two large black Labradors leaped up from the rug in front of the fire, wagging their tails in greeting, but lay back down at Mallory's command.

'Can I get you some tea, gentlemen?'

'Yes, please. That would be very kind, if it's not too much trouble,' replied Jack. In situations such as this, Jack and Bugsy always accepted the offer of tea as it gave them the chance to glance around while the owner was out of the room. There were several photographs in silver frames, all of Felix Barrington in various self-important poses. *No wedding photos or snaps of his wife on the beach in Benidorm*, thought Jack.

'He certainly fancied himself, this bloke.' Bugsy held up a picture of Barrington in a wax jacket and tweed cap, his shotgun broken over his arm and the dogs at his feet — every inch the country gentleman.

'What about this one?' Jack pointed to a photo, clearly a selfie taken in the Kings Copse. Ironically, Barrington was standing in front of the tree from which he had been found hanging. The razor wire and the 'keep out' notices were visible in the background. Barrington had his gun over his arm, together with coils of familiar-looking rope.

Mallory returned from the kitchen carrying a tray of tea and a fruit cake, much to Bugsy's delight. She put it on the table and began to pour. 'Please help yourself to cake. It was a very kind gift, one of many from my neighbours, but there's a limit to how much cake one person can eat.'

Not if you're Bugsy, thought Jack. 'May I say how sorry we are for your loss, Mrs Barrington? It must have been a terrible shock.'

'Yes.' Mallory sipped her tea.

'One of the reasons we're here,' began Bugsy, 'apart from offering our sympathy, is because the coroner has requested a statement from Mr Barrington's next of kin regarding his background and any relevant information about his health.'

'Really?' She sipped more tea.

If she's going to carry on giving us one-word answers, thought Bugsy, *we'll still be here after dark*. 'We're trying to build up a picture of your late husband, Mrs Barrington. Will you help us, please?'

She accepted the reprimand. 'Yes, of course. I'm sorry. It's just that I haven't yet come to terms with the fact that he isn't here anymore.'

Jack couldn't decide whether she meant she was sad or relieved. 'Have you formally identified your husband's body, madam?' he asked gently.

'No, I didn't have to. Mr Ponsonby, the clerk to the justices, very kindly offered to do it for me to spare me the trauma. They said the post-mortem had already taken place and it had obviously affected Felix's appearance. I've been offered counselling and they're going to let me know when I can arrange the funeral. Everyone's been very kind.'

Bugsy recalled what Clive had said about there being no MISPER report. 'Your husband had been gone for several days. When he didn't turn up for a golf match, you told Chief Superintendent Garwood's secretary that he was away on business, but you knew he wasn't. Why didn't you report him missing?'

She laughed without humour. 'Bless you, Sergeant, if I'd reported him missing every time he took himself off for days on end, you'd have been sick to death of me. And until this time, he'd always turned up again.'

'Where did he go on these occasions, Mrs Barrington?' asked Jack.

Her expression changed to one of disgust and humiliation. 'He liked to use sex workers, the younger the better. Little more than schoolgirls, some of them. He taunted me with it. His car wasn't here so I assumed he was still in Kings Richington.'

Jack felt sorry for this lady. She'd clearly had a lot to put up with. Now she was faced with two coppers walking all over her private life in their size twelves. But it had to be done. 'Where is his car now, madam?'

'I've no idea. I hadn't given it a thought. He drives — drove — a white Range Rover with a personalized plate. He never allowed anyone else to drive it, including me. It should be easy for you to find. He'll have left it somewhere, too drunk to drive. He was a magistrate, after all.'

'Where did he park it when he was at home?'

'Alongside mine, in the drive.' She pointed through the window at her small hatchback. 'Always precisely parallel, three feet apart. We have a garage, but it's quite a distance down the lane and rather too small to park his car inside easily, so he used to leave it outside the house.'

'Can you tell us about the Kings Copse, please?'

She pulled a sour face. 'It's a ghastly, gloomy place, Inspector. It had a sinister fascination for my late husband. He spent hours in there, drinking whiskey from a hip flask, taking potshots at poor little creatures and threatening anybody who tried to get in.'

'He had surrounded it with razor wire and trespass notices. Why was that?'

She shrugged. 'It was originally part of Richington Forest, but one of his cronies told him that if you fence off a piece of land and stop people going in there, after a period of time, you own it. I've no idea if that's true or not but Felix believed it.'

'Why did he want it? It's not exactly a pleasant place,' said Jack.

'You can get into it through a gate at the end of our garden. Felix said it extended his "domain". My husband had delusions of grandeur, Inspector.'

'On the way in, I noticed the empty gun cabinet in the hall. The door was open,' said Jack. 'Were you surprised when your husband took his gun with him, the last time he went out?'

She looked quizzical. 'Not at all. Why would I? He often drove around with it in the boot of his car. He liked to go out into the country and shoot at pigeons and pheasants. He enjoyed killing things.'

Jack thought he'd better tread carefully, as he wasn't entirely sure how much Mrs Barrington knew about the manner of her husband's death. He remembered Uniform saying she hadn't asked for details when they made the 'death call' and they hadn't given her any. 'Did your husband leave a note, madam?'

She refilled their teacups and picked hers up. 'What kind of note? I don't understand. Why would he have left a note?'

Jack and Bugsy exchanged glances. 'A suicide note, Mrs Barrington. The deceased person often leaves one behind in a case like this. Out of the need to explain to their loved ones why they did it.'

Her expression froze. 'Suicide?'

'Yes. Your husband hanged himself.'

She dropped the cup and hot tea spilled all over her skirt. 'No! He can't have! It's not possible!'

'I'm sorry. The post-mortem confirmed it. We thought you knew.'

'No, I didn't. When the police told me they'd found his body in the copse, I thought he must have had a heart attack or some kind of stroke.' She showed genuine surprise and distress for the first time, her face drained of colour. 'Are you saying you found him hanging . . . from a . . . tree?'

'Yes, we did. I'm sorry it was such a shock for you.' Jack was puzzled. She really didn't know Barrington had hanged himself, he was sure of it. 'Can you think of any reason why your husband would have wanted to kill himself — a deterioration in his mental health, perhaps, or any money worries? Those are the things the coroner will want to know.'

'No. I'm sorry. I can't.'

So it seemed she had no idea that her late husband had done away with himself after shooting two people dead in Richington Mallet. Jack was perplexed. The car, wherever it was, would contain a good deal of their blood, assuming Barrington had jumped in it and driven off straight after the shootings. He must have left it somewhere near the forest, then walked to the copse with his gun and the rope.

Uniform would find the car. Instinct told him it was at this point that he should ask her if she knew of any connection Barrington may have had with Allegra Parnell and Brian Roberts. But this wasn't the time — she'd had enough bad news already and she looked close to collapsing.

'Would you like me to call a doctor?'

She hesitated, as if struggling to take it all in. 'No . . . thank you. I shall be all right. I just need time to rest.'

'Thank you, Mrs Barrington. We may need to speak with you again.'

* * *

Outside the house, reporters and a couple of photographers were waiting. As Jack and Bugsy emerged, they began shouting questions and cameras flashed.

'Did he do it, Inspector Dawes?'

'Did Felix Barrington shoot the Divorce Diva and her husband?'

'What was his motive?'

'Is that why the magistrate hanged himself?'

'What did his widow have to say?'

Jack was angry. How had the press got hold of this so soon? As usual, he suspected they'd been tipped off by someone on the inside and now it seemed they were as well informed as the police. One of the photographers was attempting to get a shot of Mallory Barrington through the window.

Bugsy moved them on. 'Come on now, gents. Leave the lady alone. She doesn't have anything to say. A press release will be issued later in the day.'

One of the more enterprising photographers ran down to the Kings Copse and climbed over the gate. A front-page photograph of what he intended to entitle 'The Hangman's Tree' would be very popular with the more ghoulish readers of the newspaper. With any luck, it would still have police tape around it.

* * *

'What did you make of that, guv?'

Jack and Bugsy were driving back to the station. Jack was still irritated. 'Bloody reporters! Like a pack of hyenas. How do they get their information?'

'Buggered if I know. Juicy gossip spreads like chicken-pox at a children's party. Could have been anyone involved in the case.'

'Well, Mallory Barrington will have heard everything now, and it will be all over the news by tomorrow. What they don't know, they'll make up.'

'Yeah. But Barrington was obviously a right bastard and I'm inclined to agree with young Gemma. He thought too much of himself for suicide. Forensics show it's pretty certain he shot Allegra and Brian but we don't know why. The smart money says he'd have been more likely to try and get away with it than top himself, but who can tell what went through his mind.' He took out a bag of humbugs and offered one to Jack. 'Do you think the reason she got so upset when you told her that the old git hanged himself was because she wouldn't get his life insurance?'

Jack shook his head. 'He didn't have any. He didn't believe in it. I got Clive to check out their financial situation. The house is hers, left to her by her mother. She has an income from the same source. He, on the other hand, took early retirement from a retail job in men's clothing and applied to become a magistrate.'

'Gave him more kudos than measuring inside legs, I guess. Looks like it wouldn't have lasted much longer, though. The way he was carrying on, the Lord Chancellor would soon have had him out on his ear.' Needing a double sugar fix, he put a second humbug in his mouth. 'Incidentally, Clive has tracked the registration number of Barrington's Range Rover. It was caught on camera speeding down the bypass away from Richington Mallet just after midnight on the night of the murders. Unfortunately, Clive says the camera that should have picked him up heading towards Richington Forest wasn't working, so we lost him. Funny how they're never out of order if you accidentally drive in a bus lane when you're not supposed to. Anyway, the traffic lads haven't been able to locate the abandoned car yet.'

'Bugsy, do you get the feeling we still have a lot of ground to cover before we crack this one?'

'I do, guv. For a start, I think we need to "cast our web wider", like the old man said. It might help to have a few words with some of the working girls in the red-light district. I'll send the lad.'

'Is that wise?' asked Jack.

'I can't send Gemma, she'd tell them to get a proper job instead of pandering to the disgusting appetites of weak men, and Mitch would be scared his wife would find out and get the wrong idea.'

'You could go yourself.'

'Give over, guv, I nicked half of them back in the day. And we need to talk to the younger ones. They'd just have me down as a dirty old copper looking for a freebie. No, Aled will do a good job and they're more likely to talk to him.'

* * *

After the two police officers and the reporters had gone, Mallory took a cheap burner phone from her handbag and, trembling, tapped in a number. It rang a couple of times before she was connected.

'It's me,' she said. 'We need to talk. I'm frightened.'

CHAPTER NINE

'How was Mallory Barrington when you interviewed her yesterday?'

Corrie was preparing canapés in the ever-expanding industrial unit that housed Coriander's Cuisine. It was right on the outskirts of Kings Richington, so Jack had called in to tell her he'd be late home.

'How did you know we'd been speaking to her?' Jack suspected the rumour mill at work again.

'It's hardly a secret. You're on the front page of the *Richington Echo*.' She showed him. The headline shrieked: *Police interview the widow of the Shotgun Killer found hanging in Richington Forest*. Underneath, it read: *Magistrate, Felix Barrington, sentences himself to death after slaughtering Twitter sensation @DivorceDiva Allegra Parnell and her husband Brian. His motive is still unexplained.*

Corrie pointed. 'You could be mistaken for a boxer instead of a copper in this photo. Your nose is off-centre, one of your ears is wonky and you look as though you're about to punch somebody.'

Jack peered at a photo of himself in angry mode. There was a smaller picture below entitled *The Hangman's Tree*. 'I nearly did. The press are like packs of wolves, preying on the weak and vulnerable. Look at all this sensationalist hype!'

'It sells papers,' observed Corrie. 'And you have to admit, they're very useful in cases of public interest when you need people to come forward with information. Was Mallory able to give you any clues as to why Felix shot Allegra and Brian?'

'No. She's still in shock.' Jack sneaked a particularly tasty-looking potato cake topped with smoked salmon and cream cheese and popped it into his mouth, whole, while Corrie wasn't looking. 'It seems nobody told her Barrington had killed two people then committed suicide — just that he was dead,' he mumbled.

Corrie paused mid-canapé. 'That must have been awkward.'

'It was. I thought she was going to pass out.'

'Strange she wasn't curious,' said Corrie. 'I know I would have been.'

'Fear not, my little canapé constructor, I've no plans to top myself anytime soon.'

'Well, however he died, as I said before, she was probably glad to see the back of him, frightful man. All the same, it must have been something of a bombshell.' Corrie moved the tray of canapés out of arm's reach before Jack could pinch any more. 'I feel so sorry for her. She's such a thoughtful, generous woman — does masses of charity fundraising. She attends all Cynthia's "good works" luncheons. I heard that she's just donated huge bags of Felix's clothes to a jumble sale in aid of the Richington Youth Project.'

Cynthia Garwood, the wife of Chief Superintendent Garwood, and Corrie had been at school together. They were close friends and, together with Carlene, the trio contrived to become involved in all manner of scrapes under the guise of 'assisting law and order'.

'I wonder if Mallory's eating properly.' Corrie chewed her lip. 'Should I take her a casserole or a hotpot, do you think?'

'I got the impression that she's been inundated with food of one sort or another. Bugsy demolished half a fruit cake while we were interviewing her. Maybe leave it a while and see how things turn out.'

* * *

When Gemma called Zizi Starr to request another interview, she was surprised to learn that Zizi was no longer hiding out with her cousin in Truro, but had returned to Kings Richington and The Galaxy Boutique. She also sounded much less anxious.

'Ms Starr, there have been some developments since we last spoke.'

'Yes, I know. I saw it on the news. Felix Barrington killed Allegra and Brian and then he hanged himself. I'm glad he's dead. What more is there to discuss?'

'There are just a few points I need to clear up for the coroner. Shall I come to your shop?'

'I'm actually staying at Oak Lodge, Allegra's house in Richington Mallet. I'm trying to clean it up a bit. You can speak to me there.'

Zizi wandered from room to room, remembering the good times that she and Ally had spent there. The house belonged to her now. Allegra had made a will in her favour, lodged with Parnell & Parnell, her law firm. After Grafton Parnell died, she'd had no other living relatives.

Zizi went across to the wine rack in the kitchen, selected a bottle of Cabernet Sauvignon, her and Allegra's favourite, and poured herself a glass. They must have got through gallons of it over the years. She held up her glass in a toast.

'Cheers, Ally. You were the best friend anyone could ever have and it's because of my greed and stupidity that you're dead. I'm so sorry, babe.'

'Put that down and turn around.' A gruff male voice from behind made her jump.

She spun around. The owner of the voice was pointing a shotgun at her head. He was swarthy, dressed in bib-and-brace overalls under a shabby jacket and wore a tractor cap, the peak pulled down over his eyes.

Zizi had been so occupied with memories of her friend that she hadn't heard him come in, and now he was just feet away from her.

'Who are you? What do you want? This is a private house.' Her voice came out wobbly and high-pitched, not confident and unafraid, like she'd intended.

'Never mind me — who are you? They said this house was empty.' He motioned with the gun for her to move into the hall.

Zizi was terrified. She had a vivid flashback of when she had found Ally and Brian lying right there, dead, among all the blood and bone and brains. There were still bloodstains on the walls. Was she going to end up the same way?

'I'm Zizi Starr. This house used to belong to my friend. She died. It's mine, now, and I want you to leave.'

'Not until I find what I came for.'

'Put the gun down and we'll look for whatever it is together.' Zizi was trying to gauge whether she could distract him and make a run for it, dodge past him and out through the open front door.

He was having none of it. 'Turn around with your back to me.'

Zizi did as she was told. For a few long seconds, she waited for what would happen next. It wasn't what she expected.

'Police! Put the gun down!' Gemma had crept through the front door, summed up the situation and pounced on the imposter from behind. She grabbed the barrel of the gun and wrestled him for it, pushing it high in the air.

Startled, he squeezed the trigger and it went off, blasting a hole in the ceiling and bringing down a hail of plaster. Zizi screamed and ran to help, snatching the gun and throwing it crashing across the floor before he could gather his wits.

In a flash, Gemma whipped out her handcuffs. Her brain was working furiously. Who the hell could this man be? The forensic evidence had proved it was Barrington who had shot Allegra and Brian and now he was dead, too. Could this be some attempt at a copycat killing? You heard about such things after the press had given out details of a first murder. Nutters who thought they could get their five minutes of fame by following suit.

She pinned the dazed man face down on the floor and cuffed him, then hauled him to his feet. 'Are you all right, Ms Starr?' she called.

'I think so.' Zizi kicked the gun further away, out of reach. 'Who are you?' she shrieked at the man. 'Why do you want to kill me?'

He was winded but eventually gasped, 'I don't want to kill you. I didn't even know you'd be here.'

Gemma spun him around and looked at his face. She recognized him from his picture on the incident room white-board as a person of interest. 'Ted Jackson. What did you think you were doing? Possession of a firearm with intent to endanger life, discharging it and causing alarm and distress carries a heavy custodial sentence.'

'But I didn't intend to endanger life. Honest, I didn't. And it was you jumping on me that made it go off. I thought the house was empty and I could have a look round.'

'To see what you could steal, no doubt.' Gemma shoved him onto a chair.

'No, nothing like that. I'm not a thief.' He hung his head. 'It's because of my wife — it's because of Mary. She hasn't been the same since our Kirsty disappeared. We had her late in life, you see, an only child, and she's very precious to us. The last couple of years have been hard. Mary has changed into a different woman — panic attacks, depression, lack of interest in food, or the farm, or anything. She just sits in Kirsty's room sobbing and waiting for her to come home. Today is her eighteenth birthday.'

'What were you looking for?' Zizi's heart had stopped beating like a steam hammer.

'I don't know. Over time, Mary has blamed everyone for Kirsty running away. She said I was too strict with her for insisting she was home by ten every night. Josh was putting pressure on her to get engaged before some other lad snapped her up. But mostly she claims Mr Roberts was working her too hard because he wanted her to get into the music academy to promote his own reputation as a teacher. Mary believes Kirsty ran off to get away from it all.'

Gemma released him from the cuffs. 'Is any of that true?'

'No — not at all. All I wanted was to keep her safe. Josh loved her, still misses her. I'm sure he'd have waited for her, however long it took. And Kirsty was desperate to get into the academy and study music. Yes, she practised hard, but it was because she wanted to.' He appealed to Gemma. 'It's the not knowing that's eating away at us. If she's still out there somewhere, why doesn't she come home? It's because she's dead, isn't it?'

Zizi was beginning to feel sorry for him, even though he'd frightened the life out of her. 'What did you hope to find here?'

'I thought there might be something among Mr Roberts' things. A clue to tell us where to look for her.' He didn't sound as if he believed it.

It was, Gemma guessed, a straw-clutching exercise brought on by the eighteenth birthday milestone. She picked up the gun, broke it and extracted the remaining cartridge. 'Why bring a gun with you if you only wanted to look around?'

'Wouldn't you? Two people were killed here for no reason that I could see. I didn't plan on being the third.'

'Go home, Ted. Go home to your farm, look after your wife and be thankful I haven't arrested you.'

* * *

'Poor man,' said Zizi after he'd gone. 'I remember Kirsty Jackson from the youth project. She was a lovely girl, full of life and very talented. Not the sort you'd expect to run away. Roger used to encourage her to play the piano to the other kids. She was very popular — and happy.' She hesitated. 'Do the police think she might still be alive?'

Gemma pursed her lips, contemplating her reply. 'The missing person's file is still open. We did all we could to find her at the time — media appeals, specialist police units, helicopters, search dogs, and her details were circulated on the Police National Computer. We took away her computer but we didn't find anything on social media to suggest that she left home voluntarily and she certainly hadn't made any preparations for it.'

'So the police think she's dead?'

Gemma shrugged but didn't reply. It was almost certain that after all this time, that was the case. Kirsty had taken none of the usual things with her to indicate she was running away. They'd never found her phone and the service provider had reported that the signal had ceased on the night she disappeared. But unless they found her body, her mother would go on hoping she was still alive and that one day she would walk through the door.

'What was it you wanted to speak to me about, Constable Fox?' Zizi was back in the kitchen rescuing her drink. She needed it after all the turmoil. 'Do you want a glass of wine?'

Gemma shook her head, although she would have liked one. 'No thank you, Ms Starr.'

'Can't you call me Zizi? After all, we did nearly get shot together.'

Gemma smiled. 'You seem a lot more relaxed than the last time we spoke. Is there a reason?'

Zizi hesitated. 'Erm . . . no, not really. I guess it's because I've had a chance to unwind at my cousin's house — playing with the baby and all that. It puts things into perspective.' But her face told Gemma that wasn't the whole story.

'When we spoke on the phone, you said you were glad Felix Barrington was dead.'

'Yes — and I am. Very glad. He killed my closest friend. Why wouldn't I be glad? I'm just surprised that he was public-spirited enough to hang himself.'

77

'I believe you also had an altercation with him a while back, after he found you guilty of supplying a psychoactive substance in your shop.'

Zizi snorted in disgust. 'That was an absolute disgrace! He distorted all the facts and bullied everyone involved. He should never have been appointed as a magistrate in the first place — he wouldn't have been if his cronies hadn't supported him.' She poured herself another glass of wine and Gemma noticed her hand was shaking. 'Now — if there's nothing else, I need to start cleaning my friend's blood off the walls.'

CHAPTER TEN

'Does it have to be me, Sarge?' Aled had been tasked with visiting the red-light district of Kings Richington with a photograph of Felix Barrington. His assignment was to find out what the ladies of the night knew about him. 'Couldn't Uniform do it?'

'Don't be daft, son. Those girls can spot a uniform a mile off. They'll disappear into the shadows or clam up and we won't find out anything. Whereas you, young Aled, handsome and unsullied, look like you're still wet behind the ears. They won't feel at all threatened and will be happy to talk to you. Off you go.'

Mitch sloped up to Bugsy. 'Should I follow him, Sarge? Keep an eye on him? They'll eat him alive.'

'He'll be fine. It'll be a good experience for him. You have to deal with all sorts in this business. He can't always interview nuns and nurses.'

* * *

Aled parked his car on the corner of the notorious "Nightshade Parade", from where he could see what he would later describe as "a group of ladies in provocative clothing, being

79

friendly to random gentlemen". He climbed out and waited to be approached. He was, after all, there on business but not their kind of 'business'. He didn't want to be mistaken for a punter.

The first contact was when he felt someone pinch his bottom.

'Ow!' He spun around. 'Madam, what you just did constitutes a premeditated assault on a police officer in the execution of his duty. You can get six months for that.' He remembered, too late, that he wasn't supposed to tell them he was a copper.

'You just want an excuse to put your handcuffs on me.' She grinned and held out her wrists. 'Go on then, sweetheart. I'll come quietly.'

'When did you ever come quietly?' asked her co-worker. 'We can hear you come two blocks away.'

They were soon joined by several others, curious to see what a good-looking young man was doing loitering in their neck of the woods. Surely he could get what he wanted without having to pay for it.

'Well, now, aren't you a delicious young detective? Couldn't you just eat him, girls?'

'One juicy morsel at a time,' agreed another.

'How many of us would you like, sweetie? We can do you a job lot at a reduced rate.'

There was cackling laughter.

'If it's a young man you're after, you're in the wrong street.'

They were closing in on him. Fearing things might get out of hand, he whipped out the photograph of Felix Barrington. 'Thank you, but I'm not looking for . . . er . . . business. I'd just like to know if any of you ladies recognize this man, please.'

'Oooer,' they chorused. '*Ladies*. There's a novelty. We don't get called that very often.'

One of the older workers took pity on him. 'Let's have a look, love.' She took the photo. 'Oh, yes. We know him, don't we girls?' She held it up so the others could see. 'It's Felix Barrington, the magistrate. We call him "The Hangman".'

'Why?' asked Aled, pleased that at last he was getting somewhere.

'He carries a length of rope around with him. He likes to put the noose around your neck while he's on the job.'

The others joined in, as Barrington was clearly known to them all.

'Sick, if you ask me.'

'He pulls the noose tighter and tighter as he gets excited.'

'He'll kill somebody one day.'

'How long has he been doing this?' Aled asked.

'Years.' They looked at each other for corroboration. 'Yeah — years.'

'Didn't I see in the *Echo* that he'd been found dead?' asked the older woman.

'That's right,' agreed someone. 'He hanged himself. There's bloody irony, for you.'

'Good riddance. We shan't need to protect the young girls from him anymore. Do you remember poor little Celine? She was so terrified, she passed out. No wonder she went back to France.' There were nods and murmurs of agreement.

'Now, Mr Policeman. What else can we do for you?'

'Er . . . nothing, thank you very much. You've all been very helpful.'

Aled legged it back to his car.

* * *

When Bugsy walked through the gates of Richington Comprehensive, it brought back all kinds of memories. It had been much smaller in his day and had been called Richington Secondary Modern. It was where they sent you if you didn't pass the exam to get into the hallowed Richington Grammar School for Boys. He hadn't, but he'd always wanted to join the police service, like his dad, so he'd worked hard until he passed the entrance exam. He'd never regretted it. It was true there'd been times when he thought he might have been safer baking bread or laying bricks, but then again, he reckoned you couldn't play it safe all your life. And then, when he'd met and married his Iris, only a few years ago, he'd never been happier. He'd gained a doctor as a stepson and two lovely step-grandkids that he doted on. But this was no time for wool-gathering. He had a job to do.

He spotted a group of students around the back of the bicycle shed. They were all on their phones, eyes down and preoccupied. Back in the day, Bugsy and his mates would have been having a crafty fag. Phones, he supposed, were just another addiction, but they didn't bugger up your lungs like cigarettes. He'd given up smoking after a much younger and more outspoken Carlene had told him it made him stink.

He'd phoned ahead and the school secretary met him at the main door. She was a diminutive lady with bright, twinkling eyes and the appropriate name of Miss Bird. 'I believe one of your colleagues has already been to talk to Doctor Lambrick and the staff about poor Mr Roberts,' she said. 'Is there something else they can help you with?'

Probably not, Bugsy thought. Aled had done a pretty thorough job when he'd questioned the staff and some of the younger students. Not much point going over the same ground. What he wanted was some information that hadn't yet come to light. Someone here must have known the real Brian Roberts — what made him tick and what was important to him. It was only by knowing those things that they might find out why he was killed.

'I won't disturb the head or the teachers. I'll just have a look around the classroom where Mr Roberts used to teach, if that's all right with you.'

'Yes, I'm sure that will be fine. I'll show you the way.'

There were half a dozen lads in the music room, all aged around seventeen or eighteen, Bugsy estimated. Grown-ups in their eyes, but just kids in his. They'd each adapted their school uniform into highly stylized, personal versions. One lad sported a fedora and a single rhinestone glove. Another had a bandana tied around his head and aviator sunglasses. They all wore denims under their school blazers and T-shirts with *Best in Class* on the front. They were about the age Kirsty Jackson would be — if she was still alive, mused Bugsy.

He showed them his warrant. 'Hello, lads. I'm Detective Sergeant Malone. Can you spare me a few minutes?'

'Yeah, man.' They put down guitars, drumsticks and various sound equipment and shambled into a group around him. 'Is it about Robbo?' asked one lad, a good six inches taller than Bugsy, yet probably several stone lighter.

'If you mean Mr Roberts, yes. How did you get on with him?'

'*Gucci*. Robbo was sound.'

'The combo's shite without him.'

Bugsy was thinking he should have asked Carlene for a guide to "youth speak" before he came. Seeing his puzzled look, the tall lad explained. 'We formed this band, *Best in Class*. Robbo thought of the name. We rap, play instruments and do these really slick dance moves. We kind of blur the line between boy band and real band. Robbo said it wasn't enough to just vocalize, throw shapes and look cool, we needed to be proper musicians if we want to stay successful when we get old — like thirty or something.'

'He helped us write and produce our own songs,' added another lad. 'Robbo reckoned we could be mega if we worked at it.' Without Robbo, thwarted ambition hung over the lads like a dispiriting fog.

'He played keyboards with us. He was *lit*, you know? Turned up — bangin'. Have you caught the shit who blew his head off?'

'In a way,' Bugsy answered, not wanting to elaborate. 'Music was obviously important to Robbo. Was he interested in anything else?'

They shrugged. 'What — you mean stuff like football and boxing, all that macho sports crap, like Nigel the Knob? Nah, man. He only liked music. He was cool.'

Bugsy sensed that Brian Roberts had been a huge inspiration to his music students and his death had left a big vacuum in their lives, like the disappearance of his star pupil had left one in his. 'Do any of you remember Kirsty Jackson?'

'Yeah. She was a year above us.'

'Robbo taught her the piano. She used to play during assembly.'

'She was bloody good, too.'

'Then she just did one.'

Bugsy raised an enquiring eyebrow. 'Did one?'

'Yeah. You know — split the scene — sodded off,' explained the lad.

'Robbo was well *shook*. He was going to get her into a music academy.'

'There was a shitstorm at the time. Coppers everywhere, asking questions as if we were all sus. Course, we were just kids back then.' The lad eyeballed him. 'And you still haven't found her, have you?' It was a blunt indictment of the police and their perceived incompetence in matters that were important to young people.

'Do any of you know where she might have gone?' asked Bugsy.

They shook their heads.

'OK, gentlemen. Thanks for speaking to me. If you think of anything else, give me a ring.' Bugsy put his card down on a nearby drum and stood up to leave.

He'd got halfway to the door, when a voice said, 'Robbo had a girlfriend.' It was the lad wearing the fedora. The others jostled him and cuffed him around the head, knocking his hat off. 'Well, it might help the pigs to find out why he was killed,' he protested. 'We owe it to Robbo.'

Bugsy came back. This was the sort of information he had come to find. 'How do you know, son?'

'He used to post it on his Finsta. His private Instagram account,' he said slowly, as if explaining to a foreigner.

'And we overheard him, talking to her on his phone — all lovey-dovey.'

'How do you know he wasn't talking to his wife?' Bugsy was curious.

'Oh, it deffo wasn't her,' assured the bandana lad. 'He never spoke to her like that.'

'Mrs Robbo was snatched all right, but she was a *sket*,' added another lad. 'She came to an open day last year. Nigel the Knob was all over her like a rash.'

'Yeah, they went off together in his crappy hatchback.'

'Tell me about Robbo's girlfriend,' said Bugsy. 'Was she one of the teachers here?'

They laughed. 'You obvs haven't seen them. They're real mingers.'

'We don't know who she was,' admitted Fedora, 'just that Robbo had her name tattooed on his neck.'

'Can you remember what it was?' Bugsy held his breath while they debated it among themselves. It wouldn't have been noted at the post-mortem because the poor devil didn't even have a head, let alone a neck to stand it on.

Finally, the lads agreed. 'It was Jane — the tattoo was very small, with a heart round it.'

* * *

Driving back to the station, Bugsy marvelled at the remarkable lives of apparently unremarkable people. He thought he should probably be used to it by now, all the years he'd been a copper. So — what had he learned? Last year, Allegra had been knocking off Nigel the Knob: not a surprise, as she appeared to help herself to whatever she fancied, whenever she fancied it, and a macho sports coach would have been just her type. And "Boring Brian" had a Finsta account under the name of 'Rocking Robbo'. He'd been managing a boy band and bringing joy to the life of someone called Jane. Bugsy had a pretty good idea who she was. But how did any of this help with finding out why he and his wife had been shot?

CHAPTER ELEVEN

When Mitch and Clive arrived at Parnell & Parnell Legal Services asking to inspect the caseload, Jane Shaw had been far from cooperative. 'I believe I explained the last time the police were here — I can't allow you to access any of our files without—'

Mitch whipped out the warrant and stopped her in her tracks. 'I'll look through your paper files and my colleague here will need access to your computer.'

She made a sour face, as if she'd just sucked a lemon. 'Oh. I see. Well, I suppose I can't stop you. Come into my office. You're in the way of the clients, loitering here.' She'd taken over Allegra's office and eradicated all traces of her erstwhile boss — even the plants, though a photograph of Brian Roberts in a silver frame remained on the desk. Mitch assumed she hadn't yet got around to removing it. There had been no offers of tea or coffee, so they got straight down to the task of examining piles of old divorce papers and scrolling through the modern digital applications.

* * *

'If there's a job guaranteed to depress you,' said Mitch, an hour later, 'it's raking through the lives of poor depressed sods in the process of being divorced and trying to hang on to the few quid they'll have left after it's all over.'

'The time to worry,' joked Clive, 'is if you come across a petition from your own wife. Did you know that under new legislation, she can divorce you online and you can't contest it? It's the first significant shake-up of divorce law in fifty years. The only snag is that the time lapse between putting in your papers and getting a conditional order has been lengthened from six weeks to twenty.'

'Why?'

'Presumably to give people time to sort out the practical arrangements. In other words, the screaming rows about who gets the dog and who has to take the kids.' Clive wasn't married.

'No, I didn't know any of that.' Mitch wasn't at all surprised that Clive did. He had the kind of brain that stored bytes of information like a squirrel stored nuts. 'Neither do I know exactly what it is we're looking for.'

'Anything that might explain the shotgun killings. So far, the only connection that I can see is that Grafton Parnell had been Barrington's solicitor. But that doesn't explain why Barrington would want to shoot Parnell's daughter.'

'Constable Walker's a stupid sod.' Mitch had discovered the application from Tracy Walker awaiting digital processing. Her background information about Wayne made it clear that he'd been putting it about even before Allegra Parnell had hit on him. Having just celebrated his own silver wedding anniversary, Mitch found it incomprehensible.

'This is interesting.' Clive had just brought up Mallory Barrington's details on his screen. 'Look at her statement to Parnell, explaining why she wanted a divorce. Not that she'll need to go through with it, now that her solicitor's dead and Felix Barrington has obligingly made her a widow.'

Mitch looked over his shoulder.

My marriage to Felix Telford Barrington has broken down irretrievably, he read. But in the notes in support of a financial settlement, she'd recorded that his behaviour had been unreasonable in the extreme, and he'd made it impossible for her to go on living with him. It included sexual intercourse with other women, physical violence, verbal abuse, insults, threats and drunkenness.

'Blimey, he was a charmer, wasn't he?' said Mitch.

'Yes, but look at this bit.' Clive pointed.

He insisted on placing a noose around my neck during sexual intercourse and pulling it tight, causing me to faint on several occasions. When I refused, he would go out, taking the rope with him, and tell me that he would find other women who would not object, and pay them using my money.

'What does that tell you about him?'

'It tells me that His Worshipfulness was an arse of the highest order. Strikes me he did everybody a favour by doing away with himself.'

'Yeah, especially when you think that he was allowed to sit in judgement on people.' Clive paused to think for a bit. 'D'you reckon Barrington shot Allegra Parnell to stop her from telling people about his fetish? I'm meaning "fetish" as in sexual desire where gratification is abnormally linked to a particular object — in this case, a noose. Not an inanimate fetish, worshipped for its supposed magical powers or because it's thought to be inhabited by a spirit.'

Mitch frowned. 'I worry about you, sometimes, Clive. One of these days, you'll overload that planet you call a brain and it'll self-destruct. But I doubt if the fetish was the reason. For a start, the working girls didn't keep it a secret, did they? I expect it was common knowledge on the streets. And the Lord Chancellor, the Lord Chief Justice and the senior presiding judge were all on the point of excommunicating him or whatever it is they do to get rid of magistrates, so they'd have probably got wind of it too, along with his other misdemeanours.'

'True. It wouldn't be motive enough to shoot two people then hang himself.' Clive knitted his brows in concentration. 'I wonder if the sexual gratification he derived from putting a noose around a woman's neck extended to himself.'

'How do you mean?' Mitch, like most other people, often had trouble following Clive's train of thought.

'Autoerotic asphyxiation—'

Clive paused while a young man brought them coffee and a plate of biscuits. He guessed Jane must have relented and realized they were only doing their job in the same way that she was only doing hers. Once the lad was out of earshot, he continued.

'People who strangle or suffocate themselves to heighten sexual arousal. Apparently, when you rob your brain of oxygen, you experience a high. That's before you lose consciousness — or die.'

'Blimey,' said Mitch. 'Why would you want to do that? It's nuts. Seeing the wife in her nightie's enough for me. Wouldn't Big Ron have considered auto-thingy whatever-you-said at the post-mortem?'

'Probably. But you'd be surprised how many "suicides" are actually autoerotic asphyxiation gone wrong. It's one of the few sexual practices that remain taboo. Forensic scientists like Doc Hardacre won't talk about it outside their professional circles because they're afraid of giving people ideas — especially teenage boys. There's no way to do it safely.'

'So do you think that's what Barrington was up to in the Kings Copse? Bloody dangerous, if you ask me. Once he lost consciousness, he wouldn't have been able to cut himself down.'

'Yeah, you're right, Mitch. Too risky. The bloke was too self-obsessed to take a chance on strangling himself — he'd have preferred to inflict it on women. And if Big Ron's timings are accurate, he'd just killed two people — nothing very arousing about that.'

* * *

Two hours later, Mitch stood up to stretch his legs. 'I don't know about you, mate, but I reckon I've learned all I'm going to from these files and I've found nothing to explain why Barrington shot Parnell and Roberts.'

'No — me neither. To be honest, I could've hacked in from the station without even coming here, but it wouldn't have been legal and the boss likes me to stay on the right side of the Computer Misuse Act where possible. Let's get back to the station.'

On their way out, they stopped to thank Ms Shaw for her cooperation and to apologize for any disruption.

'I suppose we've seen all your records?' asked Mitch. 'There isn't anything we've missed?'

Her expression resembled what Mitch had often heard his wife describe as a "bitchy resting face" as seen on female TV celebrities. 'Yes, I can assure you, you've crawled over everything.'

Clive noticed a safe in the wall. 'What's in there?'

The corners of her mouth drooped even further. 'I've no idea. It was used only by Mr Grafton Parnell, for very private documents. Obviously, Allegra had access to it after he passed on.'

'Can we look inside?'

'You could — only I don't have the combination.' She looked almost triumphant. 'Only Allegra knew it, and of course, we can't ask her now, can we?'

'Do you have the emergency key?' asked Clive. 'The one that was supplied by the makers, when the safe was purchased?'

She looked blank. 'No. I didn't even know there was such a thing.'

'Can't you crack it, Clive?' Mitch asked. Clive was widely regarded as the whizz-kid who could do anything, however devious or illegal.

'I might have been able to, if it had been digital, but it's a dial safe. It would take for ever. The only way now is the "brute force" option.'

Ms Shaw looked alarmed. 'What does that involve?'

Clive shrugged. 'A drill? A saw? A blowtorch? We'll let you know, Ms Shaw.' He took a photograph of the safe on his phone.

'Typical,' said Mitch, when they were outside. 'The one place we might have found something useful and we can't get at it.'

'We will, one way or another, but we'll need to discuss it with the boss.'

* * *

Jane Shaw closed the door behind Mitch and Clive and watched them drive away. They hadn't found anything incriminating — of course they hadn't. There was nothing to find. Like the police and the coroner, she wanted, desperately, to know why Brian had been killed. The only man who had ever made her feel special, valued, had been cruelly snatched away from her with one shot from the gun of that ghastly man Barrington. Why? She couldn't believe Brian had done anything to harm anyone in his life. In her view, his biggest mistake had been to marry Allegra Parnell.

There was no doubt in her mind that Allegra was the cause of all this. She didn't know why, but she was certain that Allegra had been Barrington's target and poor Brian had been caught in the crossfire. Despite her determination to keep her feelings under control, she sat at her desk — Allegra's desk — and wept.

There was a tap on the door. 'Sorry to disturb you, Ms Shaw, it's Sergeant Malone. I wonder if I might have a word? I'll go away again if you'd rather not.' Bugsy could see in a second how upset she was, and he had a pretty good idea why.

'No, it's all right, Sergeant. Come in.' Jane decided it was probably best to get all the police enquiries over with. It didn't make her feel any worse or better. She sniffed and pulled a tissue box towards her.

Bugsy sat down in the chair opposite. 'I've been having a chat with the lads in Brian Roberts' music class at Richington Comprehensive. He was very well-liked and they miss him a lot — as I imagine you do. They thought he had a girlfriend named Jane and I wondered whether . . .'

'Yes, it was me. We met at the office party last Christmas. He came with Allegra and of course, she totally ignored him all evening, preferring the company of the other men there. I didn't have a significant other, so we kind of gravitated towards each other. I know it sounds clichéd, but it was love at first sight. After that, we couldn't get enough of each other. We had to keep it a secret, of course. If Allegra had found out, I would have been sacked on the spot.'

'I'm so sorry for your loss. It must be very hard.'

'Brian was going to file for a divorce online. It couldn't have been handled here, obviously.'

'No, of course not.' Bugsy was thinking that divorcing the Divorce Diva would have been a dodgy exercise from a financial perspective, whoever had taken it on. 'Thank you for speaking to me, Ms Shaw. I won't trouble you any further right now.'

CHAPTER TWELVE

Back in the incident room, Jack had called a WAWA meeting of all MIT officers. The aim of a WAWA was to piece together all the new information the team had gathered, determine whether it confirmed or contradicted what they thought they already knew and decide which parts of it might feed into the next steps of the investigation. In other words — 'Where Are We At?'

'First, I think we need to summarize events, so that we're all on the same page,' said Jack. 'A great deal has happened in a short time. Two people, Allegra Parnell and Brian Roberts, have been shot, motive as yet unknown. Felix Barrington, soon-to-be-unfrocked magistrate of this parish, was found a week later hanging from a tree in the Kings Copse — assumed to have committed suicide. He was covered in the victims' blood and various other bits of tissue, as was the shotgun, which Ballistics have proved was the one used to do the deed. It had Barrington's fingerprints on it and only his.'

'Sir—' Aled began.

'Yes, Constable Williams, I know your gut feeling is that it mightn't have been suicide. That's one of the things we need to investigate further.' Jack wrote it on the whiteboard with a question mark. 'Sergeant Malone and I visited Mrs

Mallory Barrington with a view to establishing the state of her husband's mind prior to his death, for the coroner's antecedent statement. It was clear to me that until we told her, she didn't know he'd been found hanging from a tree. She hadn't identified his body so wouldn't have seen the marks around his neck or the petechial haemorrhaging. The news of his suicide came as a complete shock and she could think of no reasons why he would have killed himself.'

'On the contrary,' added Bugsy, 'it was obvious that the bloke was deeply in love with himself. It wouldn't surprise me if he sent himself Valentine Cards. He behaved like the lord of the manor and treated his wife like shi—, er . . . very badly. I felt sorry for her.'

'She became ill towards the end of the interview so we didn't broach the matter of the double murder he'd committed,' said Jack. 'That will need to be addressed when she's feeling up to it, although from what the press were shouting outside, she must have picked up most of it from them.'

'It was all over the *Echo* next day,' said Gemma. 'There was a good photo of you, sir. You looked as if you wanted to—'

'Punch somebody? Yes, I know. That's what my wife said. Gemma, tell us about your visit to Zizi Starr at Oak Lodge. I'm sure I don't need to remind you that as soon as you saw Ted Jackson was armed, you should have stayed outside, called for backup and waited for an armed response vehicle.'

'Bloody hell, Gem! You total nutjob! What were you thinking?' exploded Aled. 'You could have been shot.'

She looked suitably contrite. 'I know. I didn't stop to think. There wasn't time. I didn't know who he was at first and I really thought he was going to shoot Zizi. I'm sorry, sir. I'll remember next time.'

'I sincerely hope there won't be one,' said Jack.

'What was Zizi doing in Oak Lodge?' asked Mitch.

'Allegra left it to her in her will,' Gemma explained. 'With Brian gone, it was all hers. She was making a start on cleaning it up, now that Forensics have cleared it. Poor old

Ted had just come to see if there were any clues among Brian's possessions that might help him to find Kirsty. Apparently, Mrs Jackson is going out of her mind with worry.'

'Gemma, did you get anything new from Zizi that might indicate why Allegra and Brian were shot?' asked Jack.

'Well . . . yes and no, sir. First of all, she seemed a lot less on edge than the last time we spoke. She explained it away, saying her holiday in Cornwall had done her good, but I think it was because she knew Barrington was dead and she was glad.'

'I haven't found anyone yet who isn't,' said Jack, grimly.

'There was something odd though, sir.' Gemma consulted her notes. 'When I first got there and I was outside in the porch — this was just before Ted Jackson crept up on Zizi — she'd poured herself a glass of wine and drank a toast to Allegra. I heard her say, "Cheers, Ally. You were the best friend anyone could ever have and it's because of my greed and stupidity that you're dead. I'm so sorry, babe." What do you think she meant, sir?'

'Right now, I don't know, but it's definitely something we need to follow up. Did you ask her about it at the time?'

'No, sir. What with the gun going off into the ceiling and covering us with bits of plaster, and Zizi on the point of hysterics, it went out of my mind until later, which is when I wrote it down, so I shouldn't forget.'

'This Starr woman obviously knows more than she's letting on,' said Clive. 'You'd have thought, with her powers of clairvoyance, she'd have seen Allegra's death coming and warned her.' Clive was cynical about anything mystical or paranormal, believing that if you couldn't apply an algorithm to it, it wasn't valid.

'Maybe she did see it coming, but didn't say anything. Perhaps that's what she meant by it being her fault,' said an ingenuous soul at the back.

'Note it down on the whiteboard, Gemma.' He turned to Aled. 'How did you get on with the ladies of Nightshade Parade, DC Williams?'

There were jeers and obscene gestures all around the room. Aled blushed. 'Shut up, you hooligans. The ladies were very accommodating.'

This just prompted more catcalls.

'Sergeant Malone, did you want to say something?' asked Jack.

'Yeah. Who's in charge of the coffee and doughnuts? It looks like this is going to be a long story.'

There were cheers of general agreement, and someone volunteered to go down to the canteen.

'I passed around the photograph of Felix Barrington,' continued Aled, 'and they all recognized him. He was known to them as "The Hangman" because of his liking for putting a noose around their necks and pulling it tight during sex. They were worried that one day he'd kill someone, especially the very young girls that he preferred.'

'Disgusting!' hissed Gemma.

'That agrees with what Mallory Barrington told Allegra in support of her claim that her marriage had broken down irretrievably,' said Clive. 'When she refused to let him do his hangman's trick on the basis that she'd passed out a few times, he told her he'd go out and find women who wouldn't object.'

'Bastard!' hissed Gemma.

'DC Fox, the heat from your disapproval is steaming up my glasses,' said Jack. 'Clive, what else did you and Mitch find among Parnell & Parnell's files?'

'Not much, sir. A lot of depressing stuff from a lot of unhappy people but nothing to indicate someone was out to get her. The Divorce Diva was making a fortune.'

'What might have been interesting, if only we'd been able to get at it, was whatever it is they've got locked in the safe,' said Mitch. 'It seems that only Grafton — and after he died, Allegra — knew the combination.'

Jack raised an eyebrow. 'Surely we can get it open somehow, can't we? Clive, couldn't you work your magic on it?'

''Fraid not, sir. It was a dial model and they didn't have the emergency key.'

'Couldn't we get a locksmith to open it?' asked Gemma.

Clive looked doubtful. 'Yes, but it costs and it's a long job. What if we pay someone and it turns out all that's inside is a couple of quid and a mouldy cheese sandwich? The chief super will have apoplexy.'

'Hang on a minute,' said Bugsy. 'Did you say it was a dial safe?'

'Yes, Sarge, and they can take a long time to crack.'

'I bet I know someone who could get it open. He should be able to — I nicked him for it enough times, back when I was in Uniform. What do you reckon, Inspector? Shall I ask Peter Pan? It'll only cost a few quid and a crate of Guinness.'

'Why not? Then if it doesn't contain anything useful, we won't have lost anything.'

'Who's Peter Pan, Sarge?' asked Aled.

'It's Cockney rhyming slang, son. A safe is called "a can", which leads you, in the obscure logic of the East End, to call it a "peter pan" which is shortened to "a peter". Peter Pan is a man who cracks safes.'

Aled frowned. 'And I thought Welsh was tricky.'

Jack smiled. Trust Bugsy to explain it in a way that made it sound even more complicated. 'Did you find out any more about Brian Roberts, Sergeant?'

'Yes, guv, quite a lot. You were right about him having more dimensions than we thought. To a bunch of kids at his school, Boring Brian was Rocking Robbo. He was the Brian Epstein of Richington Comp's *Best in Class* boy band. He played keyboards and he was "lit". They loved him. And so, apparently, did Jane Shaw, his wife's office manager.'

'Really?' Eyebrows shot up in surprise.

'Yep. He was conducting a passionate love affair with her. He even had her name tattooed on his now absent neck.'

'It never ceases to amaze me how some superficially unassuming people manage to lead such complicated, multifaceted lives.' Jack wondered where they found the energy.

Bugsy drew arrows connecting Jane Shaw to Brian Roberts on the whiteboard, but he didn't reckon it added much to the investigation. 'I spoke to her and she confirmed it. Obviously, she knew Barrington had killed him but she said she had no idea why, and I believed her. However, she was convinced we'd discover that Allegra Parnell was at the root of it. Incidentally, according to the boys in the band, Allegra and Nigel the Knob, Richington Comp's PE teacher, had been — Now, how can I put this without offending those of you who are easily shocked? — oh yes, practising squat thrusts together. They met on the school's open day. Ms Parnell obviously thought that applied to her legs.'

'Inspector Dawes?' said a voice, against the background of laughter. DC Dinkley, a serious young officer, put up a tentative hand. She was known as 'Velma' to her colleagues, after the character in *Scooby-Doo*, mainly due to her baggy sweaters, square, horn-rimmed spectacles and undoubted intelligence. 'I've been reading through the pathology report. It says Barrington had recent dog bites on his arm and leg. Did Parnell and Roberts own a dog? Was he bitten when he went into their house to shoot them?'

'No, there's nothing in their background information about a dog,' said Gemma. 'If there had been, Uniform would have had to arrange for it to be taken it away to an animal shelter.'

'Mallory Barrington has dogs — two black Labradors,' recalled Jack.

'Surely Barrington wouldn't have been bitten by his own dogs,' said Velma.

'It rather depends on what he was doing at the time,' said Jack. 'And on the subject of Dr Hardacre's report, we still have the anomaly around the fungus that only grows on the ground being found up a tree in Barrington's hair.'

'Sir, why don't I do a reconstruction?' Aled was determined to demonstrate that such a suicide was by no means an easy feat. 'I'll go into the Kings Copse, climb the same tree with an identical length of rope and see how difficult it is to hang myself.'

'Aled, that doesn't sound safe to me,' cautioned Gemma. 'What if something goes wrong?'

'Huh!' scoffed Aled. 'That's rich, coming from someone who wrestled with a bloke holding a loaded shotgun. What do you think, sir?'

Jack hesitated. 'I'll give it some thought, but if you do it, you're not going without backup. In the meantime, I'll visit Mallory Barrington again, now she's had time to recover. We need to get her opinion about why she thinks her late husband shot two people and how he got the dog bites. Gemma, speak to Zizi. Ask her about the toast to her best friend and her reasons for believing it was her fault that Allegra was shot. Sergeant Malone, find Peter Pan and persuade him to crack the Parnell & Parnell safe. Tell him he won't be nicked — this time. Anything else?'

'Sir, why haven't we found Barrington's Range Rover yet?' It was DC Dinkley again. 'He must have left it somewhere close to the copse for him to be able to walk there carrying the shotgun and the rope while he was under the influence, had just killed two people and was covered in their blood. You wouldn't walk far in that condition. Has anybody looked in his garage?'

'He wouldn't have put it in the garage, Velma.' Aled scanned the transcript of the interview with Mallory. 'Mrs Barrington said it was quite a distance down the lane and too small to park a Range Rover inside easily, so he used to leave it outside the house. It wasn't there, which is why she thought he was still out, tomcatting.'

'Yes, I know what she said, Aled. I read the report too. But has anybody checked? I'm sure everyone remembers the plot of "The Purloined Letter" by Edgar Allen Poe? Where was it hidden? In a letter rack. Where should we look for a car? In a garage.'

It went quiet for a bit, and everyone stared at her. She said, 'I read a lot of crime novels.'

'That's a good point . . . er . . . Velma,' said Jack, who couldn't remember her real name. He wasn't sure he'd ever known it. 'I'll take a look when I go to see Mrs Barrington.'

CHAPTER THIRTEEN

Jack could tell from her barely disguised irritation that Mallory Barrington wasn't pleased to see him again. She'd been on the phone when he found her sitting outside on a bench in the afternoon sun. He'd heard her say, 'I've got to go. The police are here. I'll call you back.'

'Inspector Dawes. What can I do for you?'

No offer of tea, this time, Jack noted. He began gently. 'I'm sorry to interrupt your phone conversation, Mrs Barrington.'

She shrugged it off. 'It's fine. It was just a friend from a charity I support. We were discussing arrangements for a jumble sale that's coming up. Would you like a drink? I usually have one around this time.'

'No, thanks, but don't let me stop you.' Jack thought she was looking very pale and thin. He would speak to Corrie about her offer of a casserole.

They went inside and Mallory mixed herself a large gin and tonic with ice and a slice of lime. 'I assume you're here about Felix again.'

'Last time we spoke, I didn't ask if you knew of any connection Mr Barrington may have had with Allegra Parnell and Brian Roberts.'

'He shot them both, didn't he?' She looked bleak. 'It's been all over the media. It was impossible not to see it.'

'Yes, I'm afraid there's no doubt about it. When your husband was found, he had their blood all over him and the forensics have proved that the shots that killed the couple were fired from his gun.'

'I can't imagine why Felix would do such a terrible thing, if that's what you're asking. I wasn't aware that he'd had anything to do with either of them, let alone wanted to kill them. I can only assume it was some kind of mental aberration. It does at least explain why Felix hanged himself. He must have been consumed with remorse once he came to his senses, don't you think, Inspector?'

Jack didn't answer that. She was holding back the fact that Allegra Parnell had been dealing with her divorce application and financial settlement, but he didn't want to browbeat her into telling him. 'Do you think I could take a look in your garage, please?'

She looked reluctant. 'But there's nothing in there except a few tools and some garden furniture. Neither of us used it for our cars. I haven't been in there for ages, certainly not since Felix died. Why do you need to see it?'

'I can get a warrant if you'd prefer.'

'No, that won't be necessary.'

Jack followed her out of the back door and she took a key from a hook on the wall. 'It's some yards away, Inspector.'

The garage was free-standing and set back round a bend in the lane. Jack could see how it would be tricky trying to manoeuvre a Range Rover inside — but not impossible. Mallory unlocked the up-and-over door and Jack lifted and tilted it. There, parked tightly inside, was Barrington's white Range Rover with the personalized plate.

Well done, Velma, thought Jack.

'Did you know your husband's car was in here, Mrs Barrington?'

She looked flustered. 'Why would I? He rarely parked it in here. He said it was too awkward. When his body was found

101

in the Kings Copse, I thought he must have abandoned his car somewhere and walked home, and that was what had brought on his heart attack. It was only later that you came and told me he'd hanged himself. You saw how shocked I was.'

'So you've no idea how long it's been there?'

'No. None at all.'

Jack knew that pretty much everything she'd just told him was a lie. She had one of those open faces that telegraphed when she said something that wasn't true. If only all the people he questioned were the same, his job would be much simpler.

He closed the door, locked it and kept the key. 'I shall need to get a forensics team to examine the car and the garage, Mrs Barrington.' Also, he didn't want to ask her any more questions without a digital recorder and another officer present.

They walked back to the house in silence. When Jack went to get in his car, she put a hand on his arm. She seemed to have come to a decision.

'I haven't been entirely honest with you, Inspector. When I said I couldn't think of a reason why my husband would want to harm Allegra Parnell, that wasn't true. She had been putting together my application for a divorce settlement. If Felix had somehow found that out, he would have been angry enough to go and threaten her. He had a terrible temper, especially when he couldn't get his own way. Maybe things got out of hand and he shot her. Her poor husband must have been a witness so he got the same treatment. I'm sorry. I should have told you earlier.'

'I shall need you to come to the station and make a statement tomorrow, please.'

'Yes, of course.'

After he'd gone, she took out her phone and pressed the speed dial.

'The police have found the car. I had to tell them about Allegra Parnell dealing with the divorce. I didn't have a choice.'

* * *

102

The car was winched from the garage onto a flatbed truck and towed to the police pound, where a team of SOCOs in white coveralls swarmed all over it like an army of ants. Their report, when Jack received it, identified considerable quantities of dried blood, skin and pulp across the driver's seat, the door and the floor. The conclusion was that Barrington had trodden in Allegra's and Brian's remains when he fled Oak Lodge and had transferred them from his clothes and shoes to the car.

In the back, they found multiple fingerprints and the detritus and DNA consistent with a vehicle that had been used by Barrington as a mobile knocking-shop. In the boot there were fibres from a twisted, jute-based rope — the same that Dr Hardacre had removed from Barrington's neck — gunshot residue and oil, indicating that it had been used, regularly, to transport a weapon. But the most telling piece of information concerned the steering wheel.

'Listen up, team.' Jack called them together. 'This is Forensics' report on Barrington's vehicle. They found all the things we were expecting. Apart from all the blood and guts, there were multiple fingerprints all over the inside but there were only two clear sets on the steering wheel. One set was Barrington's, obviously.'

'So the other set would be Mrs Barrington's,' assumed Gemma. 'Do we have her fingerprints?'

'No,' said Jack, 'but she told me Barrington never let anyone else drive the Range Rover — not even her. SOCOs ruled out some smudged prints that were too old to be relevant, possibly belonging to the mechanics who serviced it, but there were only two fresh sets. Clive, can you run the anonymous set through the database? It's a shot in the dark but we might just have a match. Barrington had some very dodgy contacts. One of his cronies could have form.'

* * *

Zizi was in her shop rearranging the aromatherapy candles in the window to showcase the ones that assisted in reducing stress,, or energized to promote creativity. She saw the policewoman getting out of her car. Gemma pushed open the shop door and rattled the chimes.

'DC Fox, how nice to see you again. Is there something I can help you with?'

Gemma wasn't sure if it was thinly veiled sarcasm or if she was genuinely pleased to see her. Their last encounter had been harrowing to say the least. 'Hello, Ms Starr. I won't keep you long, I can see you're busy. It's just a small matter that my boss wants me to clear up. When we were in Oak Lodge, just before Ted Jackson stuck his shotgun in your back, I heard you drinking a toast to your friend, Allegra. You said something about feeling it was your fault she was dead, because of your greed and stupidity. Can you remember what it was you meant?'

Zizi went pale. She took a small vial from her pocket containing pink Himalayan rock salt and a blend of calming, essential oils. She unscrewed the cap and inhaled, deeply. It cleared her head and gave her time to think. 'I don't remember exactly, but I think it had to do with the fact that I was meant to be at her house the night she was shot. Instead, I stayed here to increase the prices on some of my products. I wanted to be sure I made the most profit. Yes, that was it. If I hadn't been greedy and stupid, I'd have been there with her, and I might have been able to prevent her from dying.'

Gemma knew she was lying. It wasn't even a convincing lie. 'And if you had been there, you might have been shot too, Ms Starr. Then your profits wouldn't have mattered. Thank you for your help.'

* * *

When Jack got home that night, he remembered Mallory Barrington's sorry state and Corrie's suggestion that she might not be eating properly. 'Have you got anything planned for tomorrow, sweetheart?'

Corrie paused from slicing the crusty bread that was to accompany their one-pot chicken chasseur supper. 'No, nothing at all — apart from preparing a birthday party menu for ten, a charity luncheon for Cynthia Garwood and two shifts in Chez Carlene while she's helping out at Le Canard Bleu because poor Antoine has flu. Carlene has no sympathy: she says illness in men is just a character defect. Hopefully, after all that, I'll be able to fit in a visit to the hairdresser — that's if I still have any hair after tearing it out in exasperation when people ask me if I have anything planned.'

'Oh.'

'Why? What do you want me to do?'

Jack was reminded of something his granny used to say: *If you want something done, ask a busy person.* 'It's just that Mallory Barrington is looking a bit grim.'

'I hope you didn't tell her that.'

'No, of course I didn't. But she's under a lot of pressure at the moment. We've impounded Barrington's car, it's full of all sorts of unpleasant debris, and she was more or less forced to tell me that if he'd found out she was divorcing him, it may have been the reason he shot her solicitor.'

Corrie put a steaming bowl of chicken chasseur in front of him. 'But that's ridiculous. It wouldn't stop her divorcing him. These days, you can just fill in a form online. She'd have found another lawyer to handle the financial side of it. Did he intend to shoot them all?'

'Who knows? The man was a confirmed narcissist, by all accounts, capable of flying into a murderous rage if people didn't do what he wanted. I just wondered whether you'd have time to take her over a bowl of stew or something. I'm sure she'd be pleased to see a friendly face and you mentioned that she's part of the "good works" brigade, along with you and Cynthia.'

Corrie pursed her lips, concentrating. 'I'm sure I could find a window between the bistro shifts.' A sudden suspicion occurred to her. 'Jack, you're not going to ask me to grill her for information, are you?'

He put on a pained expression. 'Now, would I even think of doing such a thing? I realize your grilling is confined to the culinary variety.'

She was still wary. 'It wouldn't be the first time you've tried to use me as a snitch.'

Jack held out his bowl for a refill. 'It's just that the coroner still isn't satisfied with the circumstances surrounding Felix Barrington's suicide, particularly the fungus in his hair and the dog bites. And we still haven't discovered his motive for shooting Allegra Parnell and Brian Roberts. She's ordered further investigations before she'll decide cause of death or release his body. I know Mallory isn't telling the police everything, and the burden of it's making her ill. She might be more at ease talking to you.'

'OK, but if she hasn't committed any crimes and she asks me to keep our conversation to myself, that's exactly what I shall do.'

CHAPTER FOURTEEN

'Sir, you might want to look at this.' Clive had been scrolling though the national database of biometric information on people who had come into contact with the police after being arrested. 'I've found a match for the second set of prints on Barrington's steering wheel. I think you'll be surprised when you see who it is.'

Jack stood behind him and looked at the details on his screen. 'You're right, Clive. I certainly wasn't expecting that.'

'Who is it, sir?' The team was keen to know.

'It's Roger Goodman from the Richington Youth Project, would you believe?'

'Well, that's a bit odd, guv,' said Bugsy. 'How did his prints turn up in Barrington's car?'

'If they're on the steering wheel, it means that at some point, he must have driven it,' observed DC Dinkley. She was pleased that she had correctly identified the location of the missing vehicle and was hoping for a more prominent role within the team. 'But that conflicts with Mrs Barrington's claim that her husband never allowed anyone else to drive his car.'

'How come Goodman's prints are on the database?' asked Mitch. 'He must have form.'

Clive read out the details from the original charge sheet. 'Roger Jeffrey Goodman was arrested and charged with common assault under Section 39 of the Criminal Justice Act 1988. Theoretically, he could have got six months, but the injuries caused were minimal, the victim wasn't deemed to be vulnerable and the offence wasn't premeditated. Also, the magistrate found that there was a degree of provocation and Goodman got a fine and a conditional discharge. It wasn't Barrington on the bench, incidentally, it was a lady magistrate. Otherwise, he'd probably have been sent down for the maximum sentence.'

'Who was the victim?' asked Bugsy.

Clive scanned the report. 'A bloke called Nigel Knobbs. He's a—'

'PE teacher at Richington Comp,' finished Bugsy. 'The lads call him Nigel the Knob. He was knocking off Allegra Parnell in his spare time. I wonder how he got into an altercation with Roger Goodman.'

'I think we should pull Goodman in and squeeze his pips,' said Gemma. 'There was definitely something shifty about his manner when I spoke to him.'

Mitch walked across to the whiteboard with a pen. 'Is it just me, or is this case getting very confused? Everyone seems to have some sort of connection to everyone else.'

'I know what you mean,' agreed Aled. 'We started this investigation with two people dead from gunshot wounds, one of whom, Allegra Parnell, was either arranging divorces for women or knocking off their husbands.'

'And in some cases, both at the same time,' added someone.

Mitch drew connecting arrows between the photos of each protagonist as he spoke. 'Her husband, Brian, also found dead, taught music at the same school as one of Allegra's boyfriends, Nigel the Knob, who we now discover had been assaulted by Roger, the youth project leader. Brian also taught Kirsty, budding concert pianist, missing for two years and last seen leaving a dance with boyfriend, Josh, at the aforementioned youth project. Her embittered father, Ted Jackson, stalks the community, brandishing a shotgun and looking for her. At the same time, Boring Brian, alias Rocking Robbo, was managing a boy band and having an affair with Jane, his wife's office manager.'

Aled took the pen and continued with the arrows. 'We've got a magistrate, Felix Barrington, who shot the couple and may or may not have hanged himself afterwards. Then there's his wife, Mallory, for whom Allegra was also preparing divorce papers, and Zizi Starr, Allegra's best friend, who had been fined heavily by the magistrate for an offence she vehemently denies. Subsequently, Zizi has been threatened by the father of the missing girl and she is also heavily involved in Roger's youth project. And now, the fingerprints of said project leader have turned up on the steering wheel of the magistrate's car.' He stood back and looked at the board, now completely covered in crisscrossed arrows. 'Any ideas?'

'I've got it!' declared Bugsy. 'It was Professor Plum in the ballroom with a candlestick. Now let's all go down the pub, sit on something soft and give our brains a rest.'

* * *

Uniform picked up Roger Goodman from the community centre the next day. He had been setting out chairs for a parish council meeting, due to take place that afternoon. The officers explained that he wasn't being arrested but he was a person of interest and the MIT needed to speak to him again, down at the station. They put him in an interview room with a constable by the door.

'Come on, Gemma,' said Jack. 'We need Goodman to explain how his fingerprints came to be on Barrington's steering wheel. You can work the digital recording gismo while Sergeant Malone and I squeeze his pips, as you so elegantly put it.'

Goodman was concerned but amenable. 'Can you tell me what this is about, Inspector, only I'm needed at a parish council meeting? I believe funding is on the agenda, so obviously I want to be there.'

Jack nodded to Gemma and she switched on the recording and announced who was in the room.

'This shouldn't take too long, Mr Goodman,' said Jack. 'As an active member of the Kings Richington community, you'll have heard about the recent death of the magistrate Felix Barrington.'

Goodman nodded. 'Indeed, I did. I read about it in the *Sunday Echo*. It was the first time I smiled all day.'

'I take it you weren't a friend of his?' asked Bugsy.

'He didn't have any friends. But then, he didn't need any, did he? He was his own fan club. Committing suicide was the only selfless thing he did in his entire life.'

Bugsy corrected him. 'The coroner hasn't yet determined his death was suicide.'

Goodman looked surprised. 'What else could it be? The *Echo* said he was found hanging from a tree in the Kings Copse after shooting that couple in Richington Mallet.'

'You can't believe everything you read in the papers, sir. Did you have much to do with Felix Barrington?' Jack sensed an underlying tension although Goodman continued to appear composed.

'No, not at all. Like most people in Kings Richington, I stayed as far away from him as possible. I believe he had a few cronies down at the golf club — your chief superintendent was one of them, and so was Grafton Parnell before his heart took him — but otherwise, Barrington wasn't what you'd call popular. I don't think our paths ever really crossed. Why do you ask?'

Having sat in on interviews such as this on several occasions, Gemma knew that having created a cleverly constructed ambush, Inspector Dawes would now invite Goodman to walk into it by referring to the real issue that they were there to address.

'In that case, Mr Goodman, can you explain how a set of your fingerprints came to be on the steering wheel of Mr Barrington's Range Rover?'

The hush that fell over the room was almost tangible. For long moments, impending disaster seemed to hang over Goodman's head like the Sword of Damocles. Then, he struck his forehead with the heel of his hand. 'Of course! Now, I remember. Mrs Barrington supports a charity that funds the Richington Youth Project. She was planning to attend a meeting of trustees, of which I am one, but found that Felix had gone out on one of his wildlife-destruction jaunts through Richington Forest, leaving his car blocking hers in. She knew I had to pass her house on my way to the meeting and phoned to ask me if I would stop off and move the Range Rover for her as she'd never driven it and it had to be reversed at a tight angle. She said Barrington would be furious if she dented it. Naturally, I did what she asked. It must have been then that I left my prints on the wheel.'

If that was a lie, thought Bugsy, *it was a pretty good one on the spur of the moment.*

'If you were both going to the same meeting, why didn't you just offer her a lift?' asked Jack.

'Because Mrs Barrington was going on somewhere else afterwards and needed her car. I didn't ask where — it was none of my business.' His brow furrowed. 'May I ask how you came to have a set of my prints on your records, Inspector? I don't recall ever giving my permission.'

'Certainly, sir. DC Fox, will you please explain the law to Mr Goodman?'

Gemma looked up from her laptop, where she'd been typing notes. 'Under the wide-ranging provisions contained in the Police and Criminal Evidence Act 1984, the police can take a person's fingerprints without consent if they have been arrested, charged or convicted of an offence in the United Kingdom. Your prints were taken, Mr Goodman, when you were arrested, charged and convicted of common assault on Mr Nigel Knobbs, under Section 39 of the Criminal Justice—'

'Yes, thank you, DC Fox, I do remember now.' Goodman muttered an aside to Bugsy: 'Smart lady. She must be a riot at parties.'

'She has a law degree,' replied Bugsy, as if in mitigation.

'Since we have broached the subject,' said Jack, 'the common assault charge says you punched Knobbs on the jaw.'

'That's right, I did. He bloody well deserved it. Knobbs is a washed-up amateur boxer with so many insecurities, it's a miracle he doesn't disintegrate. He has to live with the constant knowledge that he isn't as bright as the kids he teaches and he resents it. I could have tolerated that, but like a lot of second-rate PE teachers who aren't up to the job, the man is a sadist and a bully.'

'What happened?' Gemma's curiosity had made her forget about the pips they were there to squeeze.

'He came to the gym one evening when I was coaching some of the lads. Pranced about like he was some sort of champion — gloves, boots, headgear, silk boxing shorts, the whole get-up. Obviously, the lads were impressed. You know the saying — teachers are men to boys but they're just boys to men. He offered to spar with one of them and picked a skinny kid half his size, one that he enjoyed bullying at Richington Comp. I could see the lad didn't want to do it but he didn't want to look a wimp, either, so I kept a close eye.'

By now, Gemma and Bugsy were sitting forward in their seats. 'What happened next?' asked Gemma.

'Well, he chased the lad around the ring, jabbing and punching him, and jeering that he was a mummy's boy and he was going to make a man of him.'

'The bastard,' said Gemma, predictably. 'What did you do?'

'Eventually, Knobbs knocked him down and the lad burst into tears. Knobbs was screaming at him to get up and fight, so I climbed into the ring, told him to pick on someone his own size, and punched him on the jaw. He went down like a sack of spuds and refused to get up when I challenged him to fight like a man. All the lads cheered and laughed at him. Anyway, he pressed charges and I got done for assault, but I don't regret it.'

'Good man!' said Bugsy.

'Well done!' Gemma was delighted. 'Would you like a cup of tea?'

Jack stared at both his officers in amazement. 'I think we could all do with one.'

* * *

After the copper on the door had shown Goodman out, Jack turned on Bugsy and Gemma. 'What was that all about? *Well done*? *Good man*? and *Would you like a cup of tea*? Did you two forget why we pulled Goodman in? It wasn't supposed to be so that you could pat him on the back.'

'I know, sir, but he did the right thing, even if it was technically an assault,' said Gemma. 'These macho sports teachers chuck their weight about because they think they're hard. They have to be taken down, publicly, in front of the lads they've bullied. Otherwise, how will youngsters learn what is decent behaviour?'

'I thought his explanation for the fingerprints was perfectly reasonable,' said Bugsy, mildly. 'Don't you agree, guv?'

'Yes, I suppose so. In any case, it would be very difficult to disprove.'

'Do you want me to go and question Mallory Barrington, sir — see if her version tallies with his?' asked Gemma.

'No, it's OK. I've no doubt that it will, and Mrs Dawes is taking her some food, so they'll be having a good chat. I'll wait and see if anything useful comes out of that.'

CHAPTER FIFTEEN

'Corrie, this is so kind.' Mallory took the containers of food as Corrie unloaded them from one of her bright green Coriander's Cuisine vans. 'I really haven't been able to summon up the energy to cook and I have to confess I've been living off cheese and biscuits and gin. Your food is always so delicious. Thank you so much.'

'You must take care of yourself, Mallory. We need you to be fit enough to help with the jumble sale in aid of the Richington Youth Project.'

'I'll be fine. Please come inside. What would you like — tea or coffee?'

They settled in the drawing room, where the Labradors ambled over and laid their heads on Corrie's knees to have their ears fondled. 'I'm sure you'll feel better once Felix's funeral is over.'

Mallory nodded. 'I shall. The problem at the moment is that the coroner is demanding more information about his suicide before the body can be released. He didn't leave a note, you see.'

'I seem to recall Jack mentioning something in the pathology report about dog bites, which the coroner wants explained. Surely not these two softies?'

'No, definitely not Bilbo and Baggins.' The dogs looked up at the sound of their names. 'I asked if the pathologist was certain they were dog bites. You see, they might have been from a fox. One of my late husband's favourite pastimes was to trap a fox in a wire cage, throw in a live rabbit and watch the fox tear it to pieces.'

Corrie shuddered. 'Mallory, that's horrible. How could you bear to live with a man who did appalling things like that?'

'I wasn't going to for much longer. Allegra Parnell said that under the new no-fault divorce legislation, all I had to do was provide a legal statement to say the marriage had broken down irretrievably. It counts as conclusive evidence and can't be contested. She'd worked out a truly brilliant financial settlement. The terms would ensure I kept everything, including my mother's house, and Felix would get pretty much just what he stood up in. Even though the new law meant I didn't need to list the grounds for a divorce, everyone would have known about them. The humiliation and disgrace of divorce would have been intolerable for someone like him. It's for that reason that I think he went into an insane, drunken rage and shot Allegra. Hanging was the best outcome for him.'

'Jack said you found Felix's car in your garage in the end.' Corrie reached for a piece of carrot cake, which she imagined had been made by one of Mallory's neighbours. It was surprisingly good and she was always on the lookout for staff.

'Yes. I can only assume he put it in there so that I would think he was still in town.'

'Maybe he didn't want you to go looking for him and find him hanging from the tree.' Although, even as she said it, Corrie doubted Barrington would have had that much concern for his wife's feelings.

'Felix knew I would never venture into the Kings Copse. It was an awful place — full of dead things, cold and rotting. His sinister obsession with it gave me the creeps. It was totally right for him to die there.'

At that point, Corrie thought it prudent to leave. It was clear that Mallory was suffering, not just from her husband's sudden death but from the miserable life he'd put her through. And there was something else, something that was troubling her greatly. Corrie hoped Jack would soon get the confirmation of suicide that the coroner was looking for, so that Mallory could go ahead with the funeral and look forward to a new, happier future.

* * *

When Jack came through the door that evening, Corrie put both arms around him and hugged him tight.

He hugged her back. 'What was that for?'

'Nothing special. Just that I'm glad I married you. After all, it's a bit of a lottery, isn't it? I might have ended up with somebody like Felix Barrington.'

Jack took off his coat. It seemed that Corrie's visit to Mrs Barrington had affected her more than she had expected. 'How was Mallory?'

'Not good. There's something weighing heavily on her and she wouldn't tell me what it was, just that she wants everything to be over. I asked her about the dog bites and she said she thought they were probably made by a fox. It seems that Barrington liked to torture the wildlife before he slaughtered it. He really was a ghastly individual, Jack.'

'I think we've all come to that conclusion. My problem is that it tends to lead me towards Gemma's and Aled's opinions that he was too self-obsessed to kill himself. Aled wants to do a reconstruction of the hanging to demonstrate to the coroner that it's unlikely Barrington could have managed it. We may be looking at another murder.'

'That sound dangerous. Look after Aled, Jack, he's had a few close calls in the past. He acts first and thinks afterwards.'

'I know, but I don't want to dampen his enthusiasm for the job. What's for supper?'

'Your favourite. Corned beef hash with baked beans and brown sauce. Don't you dare tell anybody that I cook that kind of food. My culinary cred will go right down the pan, and I don't mean the frying pan.' Corrie became serious. 'Tell you what I did notice that worried me. Mallory had some nasty bruises on her throat. They were starting to fade but you could tell whatever caused them had been serious. She'd tried to cover them with a silk scarf, but I could see them when she bent forward to pour the tea. How do you suppose they got there? She'd refused to let Felix play his macabre game with the noose, so that couldn't have been the cause.'

'I don't know, sweetheart. Maybe the bastard put his hands around her throat, instead.' He paused for thought. 'Dr Hardacre's post-mortem report distinctly said the bites on Felix Barrington's arm and leg were made by a dog. Big Ron's never wrong. If she says they were dog bites, then that's exactly what they were.'

* * *

Bugsy knew exactly where to find Peter Pan. He was sitting in his usual seat, down one end of the public bar in the Richington Arms. Bugsy joined him. 'Evening, Pete. Can I buy you a pint?'

''Allo, Mr Malone. What brings you in 'ere?' He had a sudden suspicion. 'Whatever it is that's occurred, it wasn't me who did it and I don't know nothing about it. I've got an alibi — or I will 'ave, when you tell me when it happened. I'll 'ave a Guinness, since you're asking.'

'I've come to ask a favour, Pete.' Bugsy ordered him his drink and a half of mild for himself.

Pete relaxed. 'Well, you did me plenty of favours, back when I was a misguided and confused recidivist and I needed a get-out-of-jail parole reference. I must owe you plenty in return. What is it?'

'I need you to crack a safe for me.'

'Mr Malone, I'm shocked! Don't tell me times have got so hard, you've had to turn to crime.'

'No, this is a bona fide police investigation, Pete. The safe's one of these.' Bugsy showed him the image that Clive had sent to his phone. 'The owners don't know the combination and we need to get inside.'

Pete put on his glasses and peered at it for a while, then took a long pull of his Guinness. 'Well, now, mine is a very sought-after profession, Mr Malone. There aren't many blokes around with my range of skills — not on the outside, any'ow — and this safe is a very tricky one. If you 'ad to engage a locksmith, I reckon it would set you back. . . .'

'Yes, all right, Pete. I'm sure we can come to a financial arrangement that you'd consider fair remuneration for your work.'

'OK, Mr Malone, you're on. When do you want me to start?'

'First thing tomorrow morning. I'll send a car for you.'

'Right. I'll get the tools of my trade together, and I'll be ready at sparrow's cough.'

* * *

When Bugsy arrived at the Parnell & Parnell offices with Peter Pan and his equipment, it generated interest and alarm in equal measure.

'Ms Shaw, this is . . .' Bugsy hesitated as he was unsure how to introduce Pete the safecracker. 'The operative who is going to open your safe for us.'

Jane looked worried, but shook his hand. 'You're not going to explode anything, are you? Only I don't know if our insurance covers dynamite damage.'

Pete laughed. 'Bless you, love, we modern professionals don't use "jelly" anymore. This is a sophisticated procedure requiring absolute silence, a mug of tea and a plate of chocolate digestives.'

'Oh, right.' She became suddenly aware that everybody in the office was crowding round to watch. 'What do you lot think you're doing? This is an important police operation, not a masterclass in safecracking. Get back to work.'

Pete set down his bag and took out some graph paper, a pencil and a stethoscope. 'This'll take several hours, minimum, and that's assuming it isn't fitted with any anti-safecracking technology. First off, I need to find the length of the combination.' He spun the dial several times then placed the stethoscope near the dial surface.

'What are you listening for?' whispered Bugsy.

'I'm listening for the sound that the drive cam notch makes when it slides under the lever arm. Then I can park the wheels and I'll know how many numbers there are in the combination.'

'Yes, course, I knew that.' Bugsy wondered if Pete intended to take a lunch break. Probably not. 'What about a circular saw or an oxyacetylene torch?'

Pete took the stethoscope out of his ears and looked at Bugsy pityingly. 'No, no, no, Mr Malone. That would take a very long time and advanced safes like this one are made of high-grade material with heat-dissipating copper shields. Some of 'em even have booby traps hidden inside to catch out an unsuspecting peterman. Tell you what — you can 'elp. It might speed things up.' He handed Bugsy the graph paper. 'Set me up two line graphs. Label one graph's x-axis "starting position" and its y-axis "left contact point". Label the second graph's x-axis "starting position" and its y-axis "right contact point". Got that?'

Bugsy looked blank. He was never any good at that kind of thing at school and that was more years ago than he cared to remember.

'Oh, for goodness' sake. Give it here,' said Jane. 'I'll do it or we shall still be here when the cleaners arrive.'

Some hours later, with Jane plotting all the numbers that Pete called out, he took the graphs and laid one on top of the other. Where the points met, they corresponded to correct numbers in the combination. Finally, he spun the dial several rotations clockwise to disengage the wheels, then set it at the zero position.

'This is it, Mr Malone.' One by one, he tried every combination of the numbers he'd located, attempting to pull open the door after each complete combination and spinning the dial several times in between. At the last possible combination, the door swung open.

There was cheering and a round of applause. Even Jane looked relieved.

Bugsy pulled on latex gloves and reached inside. There was a single, commercial-type envelope.

Bugsy took it out and saw that it had once been sealed and had Grafton Parnell's personal stamp on the flap. The stamp was now misaligned, indicating that the envelope had since been torn open, then stuck down again. Bugsy dropped it into an evidence bag.

'Are we not allowed to see what's inside, Sergeant?' asked Jane. 'It is, after all, the property of the company.'

'Not any longer, Ms Shaw,' replied Bugsy. 'Where the police have a warrant, we have wide-ranging powers to seize any property we believe is relevant to our investigation. I'll give you a receipt.'

Outside, Peter Pan looked disappointed. 'Well, that was a bit of a let-down, Mr Malone. I was expecting cash and bonds and gold bars. All that work for one measly envelope.'

'Look at it this way, Pete. You get paid the same whatever we find.'

'True.' He took the money Bugsy was counting out. 'Glad to do business with you, Sergeant.'

'Especially when you don't end up in cuffs getting a free ride down the nick,' quipped Bugsy.

CHAPTER SIXTEEN

Next morning, the team hovered around Jack's desk, curious to see what had been in Parnell & Parnell's safe. 'Have Forensics been over this?' He took the envelope cautiously between finger and thumb.

'Yep, guv. It's OK for you to handle. There are two sets of prints. We didn't have Grafton Parnell's on record but it's pretty certain one set belonged to him, and Allegra Parnell's are all over it. Nobody else appears to have touched it. It was clear from her reaction that Ms Shaw didn't know anything about it.'

'What's inside, Sarge?' Everyone was keen to find out.

'Well, now, it's very interesting,' said Bugsy. 'It looks like Grafton drafted an affidavit and affirmed it himself, believing the information it contained would eventually relate to proceedings in the High Court.'

'It's a legal document that he signed and dated just days before he had the heart attack and died,' confirmed Jack. 'What I haven't fully grasped yet is why he didn't make Barrington sign it, too. In it, he states that after a particularly alcoholic dinner at the golf club, Felix Telford Barrington got very drunk and confided to him that one night, a couple of years ago, he picked up a young girl in his car, bundled her into the back seat, put his noose around her neck and in the process of raping her, accidentally strangled her.'

'That's terrible!' exclaimed Gemma. The team was disturbed but not unduly shocked, given all the information they had about Barrington on the whiteboard.

'One of the working girls I spoke to said that one day "The Hangman" would kill somebody and she was right — the murdering pervert did,' said Aled.

'And did Grafton Parnell report it to the police?' asked Gemma.

'No, but he states here that he strongly advised Barrington to do so and to claim it was an accident during sex play. Parnell warned Barrington that he intended to speak to the police himself, but obviously he never got the opportunity, because of his dicky ticker,' said Bugsy. 'I'm guessing that after Barrington sobered up, he asked Grafton for a few days' grace under the old pals' act before Grafton reported him to give him time to think up a good story, or even get away. I don't reckon he ever intended to hand himself in, given the sort of bloke he was. I bet he couldn't believe his luck when Grafton — the only person who knew what he'd done — snuffed it before he could dob him in. What he didn't know was that Parnell hadn't been at all happy about it and had drafted this document in case it all went tits up.'

'Then, when Allegra took over, she eventually got around to opening the safe and found it,' decided Mitch.

'So why didn't she report Barrington then? Give the affidavit to the police?' asked Aled. 'Her dad was dead. It wouldn't have affected him.'

'Maybe she didn't want people to question her father's professional probity and, by association, that of the law firm she still had to manage. According to Forensics, the envelope had only been torn open recently, so maybe she was still thinking about it.' Jack had to try to piece together the scenario hypothetically, as all those involved were dead and beyond being questioned to get at the truth.

'At least now we have a motive for Barrington shooting Allegra,' said Bugsy. 'She must have told him she knew what he'd done, and that she was going to tell the police. He had to shut her up.'

'So why did he hang himself?' asked Aled. 'Seems pointless shooting two people to cover up a murder you did two years ago, if you're just going to commit suicide afterwards. And don't tell me it was remorse. He'd have been desperately trying to think of a way out.'

It went quiet for a bit, while they tried to work it out.

'Does it say what Barrington did with the young girl's body?' DC Dinkley asked.

'According to your "purloined letter" theory, Velma, if you look for a missing letter in a letter rack, you should look for a missing body in a graveyard,' suggested Aled, unhelpfully.

'Or somewhere very like it,' she murmured.

'Unfortunately, the document doesn't tell us where her body is, Velma,' replied Jack. 'Neither does it give us any clues as to who she was, or where and when Barrington picked her up.' But Jack knew what the team would be thinking. It was two years now since a sixteen-year-old girl went to a dance and never returned home.

It was Clive who put it into words. 'Sir, might she have been Kirsty Jackson? Going back over the MISPER report, I reckon Barrington could have picked her up that night as she was walking home after the dance. He probably stopped and pretended to offer her a lift. If only we knew the date. Why didn't Parnell record it on the affidavit?'

'I'd be surprised if Barrington could even remember the date, all those months after killing her.' Gemma was scathing. 'I doubt if it would have played on his conscience at all, once he believed he'd got away with it.'

'Too late to nick him for it, now he's dead,' Aled declared.

'And sadly, no closure for the girls' parents,' said Mitch, who had a daughter himself and couldn't imagine the anguish of losing her. 'They won't even get the satisfaction of seeing him sent down and languishing in prison for the rest of his life.'

'None of this must get back to Ted and Mary Jackson.' Jack was firm. 'It's only speculation. Without the body, we don't have any proof that it was Kirsty that Barrington killed and there's no point in upsetting her parents unnecessarily.'

'Mrs Jackson is still living in the hope that one day, she'll walk through the door,' said Gemma. 'The thought that her daughter might have died — and in this way — could tip her over the edge.'

No one spoke for long moments while they absorbed the new information. Bugsy began adding it to the whiteboard.

DC Dinkley broke the silence. 'Sir, I believe I know where the body of the young girl is.' She looked at him over her square, horn-rimmed spectacles. 'I think Barrington buried her in the Kings Copse.'

'Why do you think that, Velma?' asked Jack.

DC Dinkley had a degree in criminal psychology, which she believed gave her a useful insight into the hidden compartments of the human brain, particularly the criminal brain. 'Barrington had a macabre fascination with the place, to the extent that he went to extremes to keep people out and threatened anybody who tried to get in. Also, didn't Mrs Barrington tell us he spent hours in there, just sitting on the ground with his gun and his noose, drinking whiskey from a hip flask? The sexual *murderer* has a psychological need to have absolute control, dominance and power over their victim and in Barrington's case, this applied even after the young woman's death. I believe he was watching over her grave, sir, knowing she was down there, buried under the rotting mulch and reliving the thrill he felt when he killed her.'

'Blimey, Velma, that's 'orrible.' Bugsy shuddered. 'What's a brain like yours doing in one so young? I wonder you sleep at night.'

'Yes, but it's a very interesting theory,' said Jack, 'and it's one I think we should keep in mind. Thank you, DC Dinkley.'

* * *

'Are you sure you want to go through with this, Aled?' asked Gemma. She had a grudging respect for her colleague's adventurous approach to policing. Sometimes she even wished she wasn't quite so cautious herself, although her unthinking response to Zizi being threatened with a shotgun was probably not the best idea she'd ever had. Aled's flamboyant exploits had got him into trouble on several occasions, and she saw it as part of her job to stop him from actually maiming himself.

'Yeah, course. It's perfectly safe.'

'I think they call those "famous last words".'

Jack and Bugsy had come to observe and ensure Aled's safety under their duty of care. Gemma and Velma were there to 'make sure the daft Welsh sod doesn't kill himself'.

It was late afternoon, dark and dismal. The Kings Copse seemed even gloomier than usual. Now that the razor wire had been taken away, they were able to access it via the forest, rather than through Mallory Barrington's garden. Jack felt it would be deeply distressing for her, a posse of coppers traipsing through carrying ropes and a noose identical to the type she had seen her late husband carrying around with him.

Once inside the copse, the tree trunks stood shadowy and menacing, their overhanging limbs blocking the path. They tramped along blackened tracks that snaked through the undergrowth, their feet sinking deep into the slimy leaf litter.

'Perfect day for a hanging,' quipped Aled, cheerfully.

'Never mind joking, son,' scolded Bugsy. 'You just take it careful.' He turned and murmured to Jack, 'Are you sure this is a good idea, guv?'

'Not totally. But Aled feels he has a point to prove and since we're still having to investigate the manner of Barrington's death for the coroner, this is as good a way as any. The lad has volunteered to demonstrate the feasibility of the victim being physically capable of carrying it out. There are four of us here to make certain nothing goes wrong.'

The Hanging Tree stood like a silent sentry, challenging Aled to climb it. They looked up at the branch where

Barrington had been found hanging, some fifteen feet above the ground.

'Sir, I don't think Aled should climb this particular tree.' Velma was crouched down, examining the base of the trunk at soil level.

'Why not?'

'Fungal conks.'

'Pardon?' Bugsy was continually puzzled by this DC.

'Fungal conks, Sarge. 'They're the fruiting bodies of mycelium.'

'I knew that,' retorted Bugsy. 'Why should we be worried, Velma?'

'It tells us that a fungal infection is growing inside the tree, and not the good kind. It's breaking down and degrading the cellulose tissue that holds the tree together. It's starting to lose its structural integrity and could start dropping large branches at any time, possibly when Aled is hanging from one.'

'But sir, it has to be this tree, otherwise the experiment won't be valid.' Aled was adamant. 'I intend to place my feet exactly in the prints that Barrington made and when I'm up there, I'll see how hard or easy it is to tie the rope to the same branch that he did, put the noose around my neck and hang myself from it.'

'Shouldn't you be wearing a helmet or something?' Gemma asked.

'Gem, I've been climbing trees since I was knee-high to a slag heap. It can be done quite safely without helmets or ropes, as long as everyone exercises a bit of common sense. It isn't even that high up.'

He put the coils of rope over his shoulder and started to climb. The bark was slippery and in some places, chunks of it were missing. He lost his footing a couple of times.

'Sir, Barrington must have had very big feet — mine are much smaller,' he shouted down. 'And the indentations he made in the bark are so deep, my shoes are sliding around inside them.'

'I don't recall Barrington having excessively large feet, do you, Bugsy?' Jack asked.

'No, guv. In fact, from what I remember, he was a spiteful little man. The only excessive things about him were his arrogance and his nasty temper.'

'It's called the Napoleon complex,' announced Velma. 'It's a condition first defined by a psychological study that demonstrated how men like Barrington are more likely to have a domineering or aggressive attitude as a form of over-compensation for being physically small or short. Carrying a shotgun around with him would have been a similar indicator.'

'Thank you, DC Dinkley,' said Jack. 'I think we can safely say that in this case, he eventually met his Waterloo.'

Some minutes later, Aled clambered clumsily out onto the fateful branch. The four coppers stood looking upwards and holding their breath as he secured the free end of the rope, then he sat astride the branch, legs dangling, and slipped the noose over his head.

'Sir, if the theory is correct, at this stage Barrington would've jumped. But getting up here was really hard work and he'd have had to do it in the dark, so I don't think—'

There was an ominous crack as the branch of the dying tree gave way under his weight and snapped in half. With the rope still attached to what remained of the branch, Aled came crashing down with the noose still around his throat. Prepared for such a catastrophe, Bugsy and Jack leaped forward and grabbed his legs, taking his weight before the rope could tighten. In a flash, Velma threw off her jacket and shinned up the tree in half the time it had taken Aled. She pulled a knife from the back pocket of her jeans and sliced through the rope. Aled, Jack and Bugsy collapsed in a heap on the decomposing forest floor.

'Are you all right, son?' Bugsy helped him up.

'I think so, Sarge.' He looked ruefully at Jack and the mouldy detritus all over his suit. 'Thanks, sir.'

'You and your bloody experiments,' growled Bugsy, relieved beyond measure. 'Don't you ever do that to me again.' He stood up and dragged Aled to his feet.

Aled winced. 'I think I may have broken a couple of fingers. I pushed them under the noose when I felt the branch give way.'

'I'll drive you to A&E,' offered Gemma. She was disgusted with herself because she couldn't stop shaking at the thought of what might have happened.

Velma was back down, having jumped the last few feet from the lowest branch. 'I believe I did mention that this tree wouldn't take the strain of a second hanging.' She brushed rotting leaves and bits of bark off her sweater before putting her jacket back on.

'That was a very impressive climb, DC Dinkley,' said Jack.

She was totally unfazed. 'I go bouldering at the Kings Richington Centre, sir. I like it because it isn't just climbing, it's physical problem-solving. I could see when Aled was climbing that there was a quicker, easier way up.'

'Thanks for cutting me down, Velma,' said Aled.

'That's something I never thought I'd hear anyone say.' She smiled to herself, pleased that she'd been able to do it.

'Does anyone fancy a cup of tea?' Jack was suddenly aware that his mouth had gone dry.

'Tea?' Bugsy hooted. 'I reckon I need something a bloody sight stronger than tea, guv!'

CHAPTER SEVENTEEN

Jack arrived home late that evening, having had a few pints with the team in the Richington Arms. He went to greet Corrie as usual, but before he could kiss her cheek, she pushed him away and wrinkled her nose.

'Pooh! What's that awful smell?'

'Sorry, darling, it's been a bit of a traumatic day so I took the team to the pub for a few drinks. I expect you can smell Badger's Bottom Real Ale — it's the Richington Arms' signature brew.'

'No, it isn't a badger's bottom I can smell, it's far worse than that. It's a horrible, putrid, rotting stink, like bad meat. Even when our shower packed up during that hot bank holiday, you didn't smell as bad as this.'

'Aah!' Jack turned around so she could see the state of his jacket and trousers.

'Whatever have you been up to? You're covered in black snot. It looks like you've been rolling about in a patch of slimy, rotten mushrooms.'

'Funny you should say that . . .'

She helped him off with his jacket, holding it at arm's length. 'Don't tell me you went into the pub like that.'

'We all did. You see, it was like this — DC Williams was reconstructing Barrington's alleged suicide to suggest to the coroner that it couldn't have happened, but the branch snapped and he dropped, with the noose still around his neck. Naturally, Bugsy and I grabbed his legs before it strangled him and Velma nipped up the tree and cut the rope. That was when all three of us fell down in the mouldy black muck.'

Corrie looked at him suspiciously. 'I hope you're making this up to pull my leg, Jack, because there's no way you should have let Aled re-enact a hanging. If the Health & Safety Stasi find out, you'll be dead meat, never mind just smelling like it. What was sensible Gemma doing while all this was going on?'

Jack peeled off his trousers and put them in the plastic sack that Corrie was holding out, ready to be taken to the dry cleaners along with his jacket. 'Gemma disapproved as only Gemma can. But she did drive Aled to the hospital to have his broken fingers seen to. You know, Corrie, my MIT folks have complementary skills that make for a bloody good team.'

'Which is why you get consistently good results and why Garwood will never promote you to Chief Inspector and lose you to another division. Now go and shower — that stink is overpowering my French onion soup.'

* * *

Back in the incident room next day, Aled was sporting three broken fingers, splinted together, an outward sign of what Velma called his inner 'Action Man syndrome'.

'So what did we learn from your death-defying, free-fall tree descent, Aled?' Jack asked.

'I still don't believe Barrington could have done it, sir. Like the sarge said after Doc Hardacre's post-mortem, the bloke was unfit, middle-aged and a short-arse. I'm young, athletic and six foot three. He was also the worse for drink and I was stone-cold sober but even so, it wasn't easy.'

'So what do we deduce from that, if anything?' sniffed Gemma.

'I measured the footprints in the crumbling bark. They were made by a boot at least size eleven,' said Velma. 'According to the post-mortem details, Barrington's feet were only size eight.'

'There's something else I noticed while I was up there, sir.' Aled went to write it on the whiteboard, then remembered his fingers. 'I tied the rope to the exact spot where Barrington's rope had been tied, for the sake of authenticity. I saw scuff marks on the branch, as if the rope hadn't just been tied to it but had been dragged over it, with a heavy weight on the end.'

'I can see where you're going with this, son,' said Bugsy. 'You reckon someone else was involved. Someone who put the noose around Barrington's neck while he was on the ground, climbed the tree carrying the loose end, then hauled him up until he was hanging and knotted it to the branch.'

'But Barrington wouldn't have just sat there while they did it,' argued Gemma. 'And he still had his shotgun, even though both the cartridges were spent.'

'Whoever did it would have needed to be pretty strong,' said Mitch.

'That means it couldn't have been Mallory, although I bet she'd have liked to put an end to the nasty little bastard.' Bugsy remembered how Uniform had said she had shown barely any emotion when they told her that her husband was dead, but had been very shocked when Jack told her he'd hanged himself. Bugsy was certain that until then, she hadn't known.

Velma had been scrolling through the post-mortem report on her computer. 'Do you remember what Doctor Hardacre said about Barrington's hyoid bone being fractured? She mentioned afterwards that such fractures occur in around half of strangulations but only a third of hangings, and that scientific experts insist that fractures of the hyoid bone are almost always associated with manual strangulation.'

'So you reckon he was strangled before he was strung up?' asked Bugsy.

'It's a possibility, Sarge,' agreed Velma. 'It would explain why he didn't put up a fight during the hanging. It might also explain the bruises on his chest and the bits of fungus in his hair from struggling on the ground while he was being strangled.'

'Yes, but it doesn't explain the dog bites.' Gemma was still doubtful.

'I hate to bring us all down to earth,' said Jack, 'but while this is very interesting, it's mainly circumstantial, and such evidence must be more than adequate to meet established standards of proof. The coroner is still inclined towards a suicide verdict, particularly in the light of his admission to another murder two years ago, which she thinks may have played on his unbalanced mind. I don't think our speculation changes that, despite your valiant reconstruction, Aled.'

* * *

Walking back to the car park after work, Jack and Bugsy were still puzzling the facts of the case.

'Apart from the team and the coroner, who knows about the affidavit? asked Bugsy. 'It was very specific, that Barrington had raped and strangled a young girl — a girl that we now reckon might have been Kirsty Jackson.'

'I'd like to say nobody apart from Allegra Parnell and possibly Brian Roberts, both of whom are now dead,' replied Jack. 'But we can't discount the possibility that they had told someone else. In Allegra's case, someone like Zizi Starr, her closest friend, who was no fan of Barrington's after his blistering ruling on the psychoactive substances in her tea. And Brian may have told Jane Shaw in an unguarded moment. Both women had motives and they could have had accomplices.'

'Blimey, guv, if Barrington *was* murdered, that opens it up to a lot more suspects than Zizi and Jane — people like Ted Jackson and Josh Barker. If they'd found out about his confession, they'd both have been strong enough and angry enough to take the law into their own hands, even before any proof it was Kirsty he killed. That's besides idiots like Constable Wayne Walker, who reckoned Barrington had shot the love of his life and who's now about to lose his wife and kids as well.' Bugsy reached his car and unlocked the door. 'Talking of idiots, I'll tell you something funny, guv. While the lad was in A&E having his fingers set, Nigel the Knob came in with a broken nose. It was pouring blood, apparently.'

Jack sighed. 'Don't tell me Roger Goodman had another pop at him.'

Bugsy laughed. 'No, it was Mrs Knobbs, his wife. Aled heard her telling the doctor, in a loud voice, that she'd found out about his affair with the now deceased divorce lawyer from some disgusting texts she'd found on his phone. "Yes", she said, "I did punch him on the nose, and no, there's no need to notify the police because he won't be pressing any charges". Aled said it was hilarious because she's barely five feet tall and probably only weighs about seven stone, wringing wet. Funny how Knobbs enjoys bullying little boys but is terrified of his wife.'

'Are there any little Knobbs?'

'Yes, I think Aled said there were four, all girls.'

'Poor little sods,' said Jack. 'As if it wasn't bad enough having a dad known as Nigel the Knob, they've got a mum who punches above her weight.'

'Yes, but look at it this way — those little girls will grow up knowing you don't take any kind of shit from a bully.'

* * *

Sergeant Parsloe had just started his morning shift and had barely touched his tea and bacon roll when the delegation from Friends of the Fungus arrived at the station desk. They were mob-handed and in something of a lather, with everyone talking over everyone else in an effort to be heard.

'Please, ladies and gentlemen, one at a time, if you don't mind. What seems to be the trouble?' Norman tried to make sense of what they were saying above the din.

A chap with a bushy moustache and wearing a deer-stalker hat appeared to be the club leader. He pushed to the front. 'You need to send a team of police officers to the Kings Copse immediately, Sergeant. John and Jean Marlow have found another body. We've left them standing guard over it.'

'What sort of body would that be, sir?'

'A human body, of course. We'd hardly be here if it were a badger or a fox, would we?'

Norman was unsure whether to take what they were saying seriously or not. In his experience, avid members of any type of club tended, by definition, to be a little eccentric, but he phoned MIT to be on the safe side.

Bugsy could hear animated conversation on the other end of the phone. 'Are you having a party down there, Norman? You might have invited us, we could do with cheering up.'

Parsloe put his hand over his free ear, the better to hear. 'I've got the fungus fanciers on the desk, Bugsy. They're saying they've found another body in the Kings Copse.'

'What?' Jack was trying to listen in.

'OK, Norman, leave it with us. Jack and I are on our way.'

While they were driving there, Jack had a cold, sinking feeling in the pit of his stomach that maybe DC Dinkley's disturbing psychoanalysis of Barrington had been correct. They parked on the perimeter of the forest, pulled on wellington boots and tramped along the now familiar path through the forest to the copse.

The Marlows were sitting on a dead tree trunk. Jean was very pale. 'Oh, Inspector Dawes, I'm so glad you're here. This is just awful.'

John led them to where they had made a small excavation underneath the tree where they had found Barrington hanging. Jack crouched down and there it was, sticking out of the mulch — a small, decomposed hand, with a bead bracelet around the wrist.

Well done, *Velma*, thought Jack. 'What were you all doing here, Mr Marlow? It's hardly a pleasant place to spend the morning.'

'No, but it's the perfect site for the octopus stinkhorn, Inspector. We were poking about on the spot where it had been seen by one of our members, before Barrington chased him away with a shotgun. The octopus erupts from a kind of egg that pushes up through the subsoil in the early morning, as I believe we explained the last time you were here. But instead of a stinkhorn egg, we found this.'

'Discovering that ghastly man hanging from a tree was bad enough, but this is so much worse.' Jean Marlow looked ill. 'It's the body of a young woman, isn't it? I saw the bead bracelet on her small wrist.'

'I don't think we can be sure of anything at the moment.' Jack didn't want wild speculation to spread before a proper investigation could be carried out. 'Sergeant Malone, could you arrange for Forensics and Doctor Hardacre—'

Bugsy was tapping away on his mobile. 'Already on their way, guv.'

Sergeant Parsloe sent a van of uniformed officers who were, once again, threading police tape around the trees to cordon off the area. Jack sent the Marlows home and waited for Dr Hardacre and the Forensic Investigations Unit.

CHAPTER EIGHTEEN

The body was lying in a shallow grave. Jack and Bugsy watched as the team of SOCOs carefully removed the layer of forest litter that had been piled on top. To Jack's unqualified eye, it appeared that at some point an animal, probably a fox, had attempted to dig it up, but someone had reburied it. The atmosphere around Dr Hardacre, who was now gently examining the decomposed corpse, was even more sombre than usual. Jack knew better than to ask questions at this stage and he and Bugsy stood quietly to one side until she was ready to speak.

'You're going to ask me how long this poor young woman has been buried here in this godforsaken place,' she predicted. Leaning heavily on Miss Catwater, she climbed to her feet from where she'd been kneeling, beside the remains.

'If you could give us some indication, Doctor, that would be helpful,' Jack replied, cautiously.

'It will only be an indication, Jack. The problem is that there are too many variables that can affect the rate of decomposition to give a definitive answer. Bodies that have been dead for decades could still look fine while others of the same age are completely decomposed. But given the environment, the humidity and soil composition, I would estimate that these are the remains of a female, aged between fifteen and twenty. Cause of death as yet unknown.'

Jack could tell that this case was affecting Big Ron more than usual because she would never normally call him 'Jack' — always 'Inspector'.

'From what you can tell, Doctor, is it possible that she could have been buried here for couple of years?'

'Perfectly possible. I might be able to give you a more comprehensive answer after the post-mortem. Tomorrow, eight o'clock, sharp. Now that she's been found, I don't want to keep this poor little soul hanging about any longer than necessary.' She gathered up her equipment and turned to look squarely at Jack. 'I trust you'll pull out all the stops to catch whoever put her here.' She left, followed by the silent, industrious Miss Catwater.

Once she was out of earshot, Bugsy said, 'I reckon we already know, don't we, guv? And it's too bloody late to do anything about it because either the bastard topped himself or someone decided he was guilty and carried out their own capital punishment.'

Jack furrowed his brow. 'Either way, I guess we have to accept that we've finally found Kirsty Jackson. Once the post-mortem's over confirming her identity, we'll need to notify her parents. Best we don't inform anybody of anything until we have more reliable information. And we certainly don't want it leaked to the media.'

* * *

This decision was dramatically pre-empted when Jack was contacted that evening by a fractious DCS Garwood, instructing him to watch the local television news.

'This is a very bad show, Inspector,' he blustered. 'That damned Dimworthy woman didn't even wait for a press release. Deal with it as soon as possible.' The phone went dead but Jack reckoned he could still feel the hot air blasting down it.

Jack sat down with Corrie to watch what remained of the news from the local station. A chap with a bushy moustache and a deerstalker hat was being interviewed by Delia Dimworthy, an earnest female presenter and active member of the wokerati. Her personal crusade was to find fault with the police, the government, the council and anyone else she felt had an unfair advantage over 'ordinary working-class people'. Her current crusade was, 'The Important Question: Are women safe on the streets of Kings Richington?' The fungus club leader, whom she introduced as Group Captain Arthur Wittering, retired, was describing how Friends of the Fungus had discovered a girl's remains in the Kings Copse.

'What, if anything, is being done to make the streets of Kings Richington safe for women to go about their legitimate business without molestation?' demanded Ms Dimworthy, her bangles quivering with indignation. *'Why aren't the police dealing faster and more effectively with these sexual predators who roam our streets at will and, it seems, with total impunity?'*

Jack had been in full agreement with the presenter's campaign and her right to express it, albeit a trifle aggressively, until she went so far as to proclaim that they had found the body of Kirsty Jackson.

'Kirsty Jackson was just sixteen years old,' she simpered. *'A gifted music protégée, a loving daughter, and a friendly and happy student with a promising career ahead of her. She disappeared two years ago on a ten-minute walk home after attending a dance with her boyfriend at the Richington Youth Project. Why has it taken our police so long to find her? Is there the remotest chance that, after all this time, they will apprehend her killer?'*

'That's outrageous journalism,' exploded Jack.

Corrie disagreed. 'On the contrary, she has a very good point. Women in Kings Richington, like me and Carlene, do look over our shoulders when we hear footsteps behind us, as I imagine women do everywhere. I'm still not convinced that all police officers take the problem seriously.'

'That isn't what I meant.' Jack stood up and paced about, angrily. 'We don't yet know for sure that it *is* Kirsty

Jackson, and even if it is, that's a terrible and irresponsible way for her parents to find out. No wonder Garwood's on the warpath.'

'Oh, I see what you mean.' Corrie bit her lip. 'I've heard Mary Jackson is on the verge of a total breakdown. According to Carlene, she's taking tranquillizers and antidepressants to the extent that she can't really function anymore. Ted Jackson uses Corrie's Kitchen most nights to get them food.'

'It's too much to hope that she won't have seen this,' said Jack. And he was right.

* * *

When the call came through to the station from Ted Jackson demanding information, Sergeant Parsloe decided the Jacksons deserved more than just a visit from a couple of family liaison officers, so he went himself, accompanied by Constable Johnson and a female community support officer.

'Why didn't you tell us you'd found Kirsty?' demanded Ted as soon as they arrived. 'We had a right to know first, before anyone else.'

Mary Jackson sat in an armchair, looking vague and only slightly cognizant. The PCSO made straight for the kitchen to provide the ubiquitous panacea — a cup of tea.

Ted sat down himself and motioned to the two officers to do the same. 'The wife has been going out of her mind, expecting our Kirsty to come home. Now she finds out she's been buried in the Kings Copse for two years then dug up by a crowd of fungus fanciers.'

Parsloe could only apologize and felt very sorry for them both. 'It should never have happened like this, Mr Jackson. You would have been the first to be informed, once the pathologist had confirmed her identity tomorrow morning at the post-mortem.'

He spoke a quiet aside to Constable Johnson, who was equally regretful. 'Unfortunately, Flying Officer Farnsbarns took it upon himself to contact the media for his five minutes of fame. It's probably the most important he's felt since retiring from the RAF.'

'Post-mortem?' Mary's voice sounded weak and confused. 'I want to see her. I want to see Kirsty.'

'You shall, Mrs Jackson. Best you let the pathologist see her first, so that we have more information to give you. I expect you'll have a lot of questions.'

'Too bloody right, we do,' sobbed Ted.

* * *

Jack hated post-mortems. The disinfectant smell and morbid atmosphere of the cold, white-tiled examination room always stuck in his throat and made him nauseous. But as a murder investigation officer, it was part of his job. All post-mortems were important, but this one particularly so. Even allowing for Ms Dimworthy's persistent and often unwarranted condemnation of all activities by the Kings Richington police, he had to concede that they hadn't handled this at all well.

Dr Hardacre was standing over the pitifully small cadaver on her examination table, speaking into a microphone suspended above her head. Jack gulped back the familiar urge to vomit and even Bugsy looked pale.

'Well, gentlemen, now that I've had the chance to have a proper look, carry out some tests and harvest some DNA, I can tell you quite a lot more about this young lady. Some of my findings are unexpected but I can assure you that they have been checked and double-checked and they are as accurate as they can be.'

'We would never doubt that, Doctor,' said Jack.

We wouldn't dare, thought Bugsy.

'The deceased, as I mentioned initially, was a young woman aged between fifteen and twenty but I now believe she's closer to the lower end of that scale. From the condition of her bones and teeth and such soft tissue that remains, she was poorly nourished, with vitamin and calcium deficiencies. I also found indicators of the effects of Hepatitis B.'

140

Both Jack and Bugsy were surprised at that, since she had come from a loving, supportive home on a farm. Jack wondered if she may have had an eating disorder, sometimes suffered by teenage girls. Hepatitis was unexpected but it was readily transmissible. He supposed she could have got it from Josh Barker, but then, where would he have caught it?

Big Ron took off her mask. 'But you haven't come here for a lecture on extreme decomposition, the effects of exposure to the environment or the erosion of skeletal elements, so I'll confine myself to what you really want to know. For a start, the cause of death. She had been strangled. Her hyoid bone was fractured and I found minute fibres of rope around the neck of the deceased, which matched the rope I removed from around Felix Barrington's neck, after he was taken down from the tree. You will draw your own conclusions from that.'

Jack and Bugsy exchanged glances. 'So the evil bastard strangled her with the rope he carried around in his car,' said Bugsy.

'I think that is a reasonable deduction, Sergeant, and I stand by my original opinion that she has been dead for some time – between eighteen months and two and a half years. This next discovery may surprise you. She was in the early stages of pregnancy when she died. Obviously, the foetus was mostly putrefied but I was still able find sufficient evidence.'

'Blimey, that must have been the boyfriend's, Josh Barker. I wonder if he knew,' said Bugsy.

'More to the point, I wonder if her parents knew.' Jack thought that such a discovery might cause Mary Jackson to lose what was left of her reason. A dead grandchild, as well as a dead daughter. 'Well, thank you, Doctor. I guess that's all we need to know. It's just a case of deciding how best to break it to her next of kin.' They turned to leave but before they reached the door, Dr Hardacre called them back.

'Whoa! Hold your horses. I haven't told you the most important fact yet. Actually, I thought by now you might have worked it out for yourselves.'

They looked at her expectantly. What more could there be? It was a sad and wicked end to a promising young life, snuffed out by a sexual predator.

Dr Hardacre delivered her last and most significant finding. 'The deceased is not Kirsty Jackson.'

The room went very quiet as this information sank in.

Then Bugsy blurted out, 'Are you sure, Doc?' Even as he said it, he knew it was a mistake.

Dr Hardacre fixed him with a glare that had she been Medusa, would have turned him to stone. 'How long have we known each other, Sergeant Malone?' Before he could answer, she continued, 'When have you found me to be wrong about something as basic and relevant as the identity of a corpse?'

'Never, Doc. I'm sorry. It just slipped out.'

'Well, I suggest you keep it better contained in future.'

Jack was on the back foot. It seemed that their all-too-obvious and rather risky assumptions that the corpse was Kirsty Jackson had been wrong. He cursed himself. *That's what happens when you follow a predictable line of investigation and ignore Sod's Law. It creeps up and kicks you in the teeth.* 'Do we have any clues as to the real identity of this young woman, Doctor?'

'Yes, but I'll need to obtain a DNA comparison before I can be absolutely sure.' She picked up a handbag that had been placed inside a forensic container. 'SOCOs found this buried underneath her body. I say "buried" — it looked more like the killer had just hollowed out a trench, thrown in the bag and the body and chucked forest litter over it. The bag is cheap plastic, available in any department store, but this was inside it.' She held up the object and waited for them to respond.

'It's a passport,' conjectured Bugsy, nervously.

'Well done, Sergeant. It's badly damaged from two years underground but the plastic handbag, being non-biodegradable, meant it was preserved to the extent that some of the information could be restored by the clever forensic people. It belongs to Celine Dubois, French nationality, born in Marseilles, and her date of birth corresponds to the estimated age of the corpse.'

Jack and Bugsy looked nonplussed. 'Do we know anything else about this young woman, Doc? How she came to be strangled by Barrington? And what she was doing in Kings Richington, two years ago?'

'I rather think that's your job, gentlemen. When you've provided me with some DNA samples, I can prove irrefutably that the body is that of Celine Dubois. Then, perhaps, the correct relatives can be informed of their loss.'

CHAPTER NINETEEN

A family liaison officer was dispatched immediately to the farm of Ted and Mary Jackson. She was to explain that the body found in the Kings Copse — declared on live TV by Delia Dimworthy to be that of their missing daughter — was incorrect. Jack intended to visit them in person to apologize once again for their distress. But right now, back in the incident room, it was his job to explain the results of the post-mortem to the team.

He crossed out the name of Kirsty Jackson and wrote 'Celine Dubois' underneath the photograph on the whiteboard. 'This is who we believe the Marlows found buried in the copse.'

It was a while before anyone spoke, processing the game-changing information. 'Not Kirsty Jackson, then, sir?'

'No. And thanks to an investigative journalist looking to make a name for herself, we've put Mary Jackson through hell.' Bugsy was angry — something that didn't happen very often.

'How do we know it's Celine Dubois, sir?' asked Gemma.

'Forensics found her passport in a handbag buried with her. She was born in France and was about the same age as Kirsty. We also have an image of the distinctive bracelet she was wearing.' Jack pinned it to the board. 'She was pregnant at the time of her death and it's pretty certain she was strangled by Barrington with his signature weapon of choice — a noose. What we need to find out is how she crossed his path and where her next of kin and the father of her unborn child might be.'

'I've just trawled the MISPER records from two years ago, sir,' said Clive. 'Nobody called Celine Dubois was reported missing in the UK. I could open it up to the French authorities.'

'I'm sure I've seen those chakra bead bracelets in Zizi Starr's shop. I wonder if she was selling them two years ago.' Gemma decided to check.

'Perhaps we should speak to Roger Goodman,' suggested Mitch. 'She was the right age to have maybe spent some time at his Richington Youth Project back then.'

'Good thinking. Somebody somewhere must be missing this young woman. We need to get it right this time.'

'Sir—' Aled had been unusually silent. 'I've just been trying to think where I'd heard that name recently. I've just remembered. One of the ladies on Nightshade Parade mentioned it.'

'It isn't a very common name in Kings Richington, son. What did she say about her?'

'Celine was a sex worker — a very young one. It was after they had identified Barrington as "The Hangman" from his photograph and we were discussing his perversion. One of the older ladies said she was glad he was dead, because now they wouldn't have to protect the younger girls from him. She said that back when "poor little Celine" had been working the Parade, she'd been terrified of him because he'd put his rope around her throat and squeezed until she'd fainted.'

'Go on, son. What else do you remember?' encouraged Bugsy.

'I've got it!' Aled was triumphant. 'She said, "no wonder she went back to France". Only she hadn't, had she? Barrington had picked her up in his car, driven off with her and killed her.'

'And her unborn child,' added Gemma. 'It explains why she had her passport in her bag — she was planning to go home to have her baby. Poor kid. She must have been so scared. It's a good job Barrington's dead or I'd be tempted to finish him off myself. Slowly and painfully.'

Jack really believed she was capable of it, aided by all the other women in the room. 'We have to assume that somewhere in France, there's a Monsieur and Madame Dubois wondering why their daughter stopped answering her phone or sending them messages. She was very young to be away from home and in a foreign country. If her parents had been sending her money, there must have been an address. Aled, go back to Nightshade Parade and see if you can find the worker who told you about Celine. Ask where she lived when she was here in Richington and whether she knows the address of her family in France. We need to get some DNA so that we can prove she's the girl in the Kings Copse, before we tell her parents and make the same mistake again.'

'And in the meantime, Kirsty Jackson is still missing.' Velma, the psychoanalyst, had that expression that usually meant something complex was going on inside her head.

* * *

DC Fox pushed open the door of The Galaxy Boutique and once more, the chimes over the door insisted they were maximizing the flow of chi while announcing her presence. The scents of ylang-ylang, lavender and neroli oils hung in the air. Gemma produced her warrant card.

'Yes, I know who you are,' said Zizi, shortly. 'I should do by now. What is it this time?'

Gemma took out her phone and showed her the image of the chakra bead bracelet on Celine's dead wrist. 'Were you selling these bracelets around two years ago?'

'Yes, I still do. They're a very popular line.' She pointed to a stand where similar items were displayed. She looked again at the image. 'Is that one of my bracelets on the wrist of a dead person?'

'Yes. We believe this individual may have bought it here.'

Zizi grimaced. 'Well, I hope you don't expect me to remember after two years. Hundreds, maybe even thousands of customers will have come and gone in that time.'

'No, it's just that we're unable to establish her identity conclusively and every piece of information adds to the picture. Thank you.' As she turned to go, Zizi stopped her.

'Is the investigation into Allegra's death over? I mean, there's no doubt that Barrington shot her and Brian, is there? It said so in the *Echo*.'

It never ceased to puzzle Gemma that the public in general preferred to believe what they saw in the media rather than information that came from official sources. She supposed it was the age-old suspicion of a dastardly 'establishment' conspiracy to withhold the truth from 'ordinary' folk. 'I believe the coroner has released their bodies for the funerals,' said Gemma. 'Will you be taking care of Allegra's?'

'Yes, it's the least I can do.' She hesitated, choosing her words with care. 'Have the police established why Barrington killed them?'

'Er . . . not yet, but we're getting close. Do you have any information to help with that?'

'No, none at all.' Zizi looked as if she was about to burst into tears, so Gemma left her to her private grief.

* * *

When Aled returned to Nightshade Parade that evening, he was greeted like a regular customer, which was disconcerting. At least, he thought, his old mum, back in Pontypridd, wasn't likely to find out. He spotted the lady he'd come to find, standing on the pavement with her head inside the car of a kerb-crawler, talking to the driver. Fortunately, they didn't come to any arrangement and the punter drove away.

'Hello again, Detective.' She greeted Aled as he approached. 'Is it more information you're after or have you come for business this time?'

'Information, please,' he replied hastily.

'Well, I hope it won't take long. Only I'm trying to earn a living here, and you'll scare the customers away.'

Aled could see her point. 'Can I buy you a meal while we talk?'

'Yes, OK, why not? A girl has to eat.' She indicated a greasy spoon on the corner of the Parade.

Once inside, Aled ordered two all-day breakfasts, which consisted of a large plateful of pretty much anything that could be immersed in fat and fried — including some things he didn't even recognize. The meals were accompanied by two large, chipped mugs of weak tea.

'My name's Bambi,' she said, between mouthfuls.

'Really?'

'No, not really. But in this game, you never give anybody your real name, especially not the Old Bill. What do I call you?'

'Er . . . DC Williams.' Aled thought it best to keep things official.

'OK, DeeCee, what do you want to know this time?' She motioned to the café owner for more toast.

'Do you remember when we last spoke, and you identified Felix Barrington as "The Hangman"? You mentioned that a young girl called Celine was terrified of him.'

'Yes, because the filthy animal nearly strangled her.'

Aled thought it best not to divulge that the police believed he'd finally succeeded. 'Can you tell me anything about Celine?'

She looked thoughtful. 'Not much. It must be a couple of years since she left to go back to France. I know she came to the UK looking for work as an au pair or a waitress but couldn't find anything, so she ended up on the game. She was very young, about sixteen or seventeen, so she was very popular with a certain type of client. She used to dress up like a schoolgirl or a maid. They loved her French accent.'

'Do you know where she lived while she was in Kings Richington?'

'Yes, we got her into the YMCA down the end of the high street. Kids under the age of eighteen have to have permission from a legal guardian to stay unaccompanied, and of course, Celine didn't have one, so I said I was her aunt.'

Aled knew she hadn't had any possessions with her when they found her, apart from the handbag and her passport, but he thought it highly unlikely the hostel would have kept any of her stuff that would be suitable for a DNA sample — not after all this time. 'What about her family in France? Do you have a forwarding address?'

'She didn't have any family. She was an orphan, brought up in a convent — Sisters of Saint Somebody-or-other. When she reached sixteen, she had to leave, she said, so she came to the UK for a fresh start and to find work. But after her experience with The Hangman, she said she was going back to France because British men were "foo", whatever that means.' She looked at the cakes in a cabinet on the counter. 'No chance of a slice of fruit cake, I suppose?'

'Yes, of course.' Aled went to get some and put the plate in front of her. 'Did you know Celine was pregnant?'

A shadow fell across her face. 'No, I didn't know that. Poor little cow. She never said anything. I'd have helped her if I'd known. So I guess she went back to France to have her baby. It'll be a toddler by now.' She went quiet for several moments. Aled decided that there was nothing to be gained by telling her that Celine and her baby were both dead. 'Well, this won't do.' She scooped up the last crumbs of cake and shovelled them into her mouth. 'Back to work. Thanks for the food.' She stood up to leave.

'Thank you . . . er . . . Bambi, you've been very helpful,' said Aled.

* * *

Back at the station, Aled reported that his efforts to trace Celine's movements had come to a dead end. 'Her colleagues on the Parade and the people at the YMCA hostel thought she'd gone back to France, so they had no reason to report her missing. The nuns at the convent thought she'd gone abroad to find work, so they wouldn't have either. She could have vanished off the face of the earth with no one being any the wiser.'

'That's terrible,' said Gemma. 'Barrington just picked her off and killed her and nobody knew or cared.'

'Yes,' said Jack. 'If he hadn't boasted to Grafton Parnell that he'd "killed some little tart" after that boozy dinner at the golf club, he'd have been in the clear.'

'And he wouldn't have needed to shoot Allegra and Brian,' added Bugsy.

'Or hang himself,' said Mitch.

'Sir, I still don't believe he did hang himself,' persisted Aled.

'Neither do I, sir.' Velma looked even more profound than usual behind the square, horn-rimmed spectacles. 'Scientific studies have identified that suicide is motivated mostly by unbearable psychological pain. It's the demons in your head that you have to fight — stress, loneliness, low self-esteem, anxiety, rejection, helplessness and hopelessness, all leading to depression and often alcoholism. Barrington's personality traits and behaviours didn't indicate any of these, apart from the alcoholism. His only concern was to satisfy his depraved sexual urges, and then to get away with the murder that had resulted from them. The man was a narcissist, displaying the classic pattern of arrogance, lack of consideration for others and an excessive need for admiration.'

'If that translates to cocky, manipulative, egotistical, ruthless and homicidal, then I totally agree,' said Gemma.

'So between Aled's physical reconstruction and Velma's psychological analysis, we have to accept that it's going to be difficult to find sufficient evidence to satisfy a coroner's verdict of suicide.' Jack decided that it was time to go home.

CHAPTER TWENTY

'How did I get this so wrong?' Jack was pacing up and down the kitchen with Corrie dodging around him whenever she needed to get to the cooker.

'You didn't get it wrong, darling,' she soothed. 'Well, not all of it. I grant you, getting the identity of the corpse wrong could be seen as a monumental cock-up, and believing that Felix Barrington was the type to commit suicide, then letting Aled risk his neck disproving it was a massive error of judgement, but apart from that, you did a good job.'

'I'm not even sure what I'm investigating anymore.' He ran anxious fingers through his hair. 'Two years ago, Barrington strangled a young sex worker and buried her — fact. Then, much later, Allegra finds her dead father's statement and tells Barrington she knows — fact. Barrington shoots her and by association, her husband — fact. We found him hanging in the Kings Copse — fact. And we still have no idea what happened to Kirsty Jackson.'

Corrie paused in the process of grilling plump, home-made pork and apple sausages. 'That second "fact" — are you *sure* it was Allegra who told Barrington she knew he'd committed rape and murder?'

He looked nonplussed. 'It had to be. Why else would he have shot her?'

'Suppose it was someone anonymous, trying to get money out of him, and he just assumed it was Allegra. It would have been a reasonable assumption, her being Grafton Parnell's daughter. Maybe he shot the wrong person.'

'You mean Allegra might have told someone else what she knew and they were blackmailing him?'

'I don't know, I'm just running it up the flagpole as a possibility. You don't have to salute. Now, stop pacing about and stay focused. You already know that Barrington was guilty of three murders — the last two in order to cover up the first — but unfortunately, he's beyond justice. What you don't know is whether he committed suicide or somebody bumped him off and made it look like suicide. That's what you need to investigate.' She picked up a warm sausage, dipped it in creamy mashed potato and bit off the end.

'Are we having sausage and mash?' Jack asked. The aroma was reminding him he'd skipped lunch and he was ravenous.

'You are — I'm having a salad. I need to lose some weight.'

'But you just ate half a sausage,' protested Jack.

'As a chef, I'm obliged to taste food before I serve it, to check seasoning, acidity levels, important stuff like that.' She ate the other half.

* * *

While Jack was enjoying his sausage and mash, Velma was visiting the Richington Youth Project to find out if there had been any possible contact by Celine Dubois before her death. She was pleasantly surprised. She imagined she'd find a lot of bored teens sent there by their parents to "keep them off the streets", as Sergeant Malone had experienced. Instead, it seemed that Roger Goodman encouraged the youngsters to decide and plan their own activities. She noticed a drama group in progress being directed and filmed by another technical group. Elsewhere in the hall, workshops had been set up by the kids to learn about the environment, cook their own food and design software programmes. In the skills corner, she could see young men and women learning the basic principles of plumbing and electricity.

Seeing a new face, Roger went across to greet her. 'Hello. Welcome to our youth project. How can I help?'

Velma showed him her warrant. 'I'm DC Dinkley from Kings Richington MIT. I wonder if I might ask you a few questions, if you're not too busy.'

'Certainly.' He took her across to the hospitality corner, where there were upcycled tables and chairs designed and restored by the youngsters. He saw Velma looking around with approval. 'Don't tell me, DC Dinkley. You were expecting ping-pong, pop music and orange squash.'

She smiled. 'Something like that. It's very impressive.'

'Here, we're endeavouring to help young people to build life skills, develop healthy relationships and make decisions that are right for them. If you try to manipulate them into preconceived and outdated activities, they simply stop turning up.'

Velma was to remember those words much later, when they became starkly relevant.

Goodman indicated a morose young man sitting at a computer. 'Take young Josh Barker over there. Two years ago, his girlfriend, soon to be his fiancée, disappeared. He was devastated. His parents are very religious and told him to pray for her safe return, but as a secular young man, that didn't help him come to terms with it at all. We're trying to give him as much support as we can, but he's still suffering, poor lad.'

Velma could see that. The psychologist in her wanted to talk to him, but that wasn't what she'd been tasked with.

'I seem to be very popular with the police, lately,' joked Goodman. 'Your DC Fox was here, asking about Zizi Starr, then I got pulled in to the station and questioned about my fingerprints. Now, here you are, DC Dinkley. What can I do for you?'

'I've come to ask if you remember a young French girl coming here. That would have been around two years ago, too. Her name was Celine Dubois.'

Roger shook his head. 'It isn't ringing any bells, and I think I'd remember a name like that. Sorry.' He thought for a bit. 'Is this girl missing, too?'

'Not any longer. I'm afraid she's dead,' said Velma. 'Well, thank you, Mr Goodman, I won't take up any more of your time. It was a long shot, but they sometimes pay off.' She had watched his reaction closely and was pretty sure he was telling the truth. He'd never heard of Celine. She thought it unlikely that a young sex worker would have found her way to a youth project, anyway. No doubt she saw herself as an experienced woman, not a youngster. What a terrible way to end her life and no chance of any DNA to prove her identity, not that there was much doubt.

On her way out, a couple of young women accosted her. 'Hello, miss. You're a copper, aren't you? You don't half look like Velma Dinkley in *Scooby-Doo*.'

Velma smiled. 'Yes, so I'm told.'

'Are you here about Kirsty Jackson?'

'Why would you think that?' Velma was intrigued. 'Do you know anything about Kirsty?'

They exchanged glances. 'Only that the story Josh Barker told everyone is rubbish.'

Velma was immediately on the alert. 'In what way?'

'He reckoned they were going to get engaged when she was eighteen. He said they were going get married, run the farm with her mum and dad and have lots of kids.'

'And weren't they?'

'Not according to Kirsty. She was going to dump him. He was too possessive and old-fashioned, she said. "Completely out of touch with the aspirations of the modern woman" was how she put it. She'd read it in a magazine. They had loads of rows about it. We heard some of them.'

'That's right,' said the other girl. 'Mr Roberts, her music teacher, was going to get her into some posh academy. She wanted a career as a concert pianist. She said she had no intention of ending up like her mother, milking cows and feeding chickens for the rest of her life.'

'So why didn't she go to the audition?' asked Velma.

'Dunno. It was definitely what she wanted. We thought it was weird at the time, didn't we? Course, we were just little kids back then. We're sixteen now, the same age she was when she went off.'

The other girl nodded. 'Maybe she met some celebrity entrepreneur or a premiership footballer and he drove off with her in his Maserati.' She sighed. 'That's what's going to happen to me.'

'In your dreams,' said her friend. They giggled. 'Gotta go, miss. It's our fashion demonstration. I'm wearing my own creation. One day I'm going to be as famous as Stella McCartney and Victoria Beckham.'

Velma was both amused and interested in the vastly different ambitions of the two friends. That often caused conflict in personal relationships. It had certainly been worth giving up her evening at the bouldering centre, because although the Celine Dubois inquiry had drawn a blank, this was information they hadn't heard before. She would share it with the team next day. She felt it warranted bringing Josh Barker in and questioning him again about the disappearance of Kirsty Jackson.

* * *

Next morning, Jack felt it was important that he went to see Ted and Mary Jackson. He needed to apologize for the roller coaster of emotions they must have gone through, first being told on the television news that their daughter's body had been found and then finding out it was actually someone else. To be fair, it hadn't been entirely the fault of the police, but all the same, he felt responsible.

He wasn't looking forward to it. He remembered how Norman Parsloe had described Mary Jackson the last time he'd seen her — her face white and drawn from two years of fitful sleep, a cocktail of drugs and sheer, relentless heartbreak. As he drove up the rocky, rutted lane to the farm, he could see her in the distance throwing food to the hens. He was surprised because the report he'd had from Corrie was that she could barely function and that Ted was getting their food from Corrie's Kitchen takeaway. He parked outside the farm gate and went in.

'Mrs Jackson? Please excuse the intrusion. I'm Detective Inspector Jack Dawes from Kings Richington MIT. I've come to say how very sorry I am for any distress you've been caused as a result of the misinformation.'

She turned and smiled. 'Oh, but it's all right now, isn't it? The body you found wasn't Kirsty. That means she's still alive and now she'll have seen the report on the news. Wherever she is, she'll come home. I've been getting her room ready, fresh sheets, all her teddy bears on her bed, and I washed the curtains. She'll be upset that Mr Roberts has passed away but she's a lovely little pianist — she can play all the tunes. We'll soon find somebody else to teach her. Won't you come inside and have some tea?'

It was as if, Jack thought, as long as she kept saying it, it had to be true. He felt desperately sorry for her. Even though the dead girl wasn't Kirsty, he knew it was highly unlikely that she was still alive.

'What do you want? Why are you upsetting Mrs Jackson?' Josh appeared as if from nowhere. His voice was harsh and aggressive.

Mary put a hand on his arm. 'It's all right, Josh. The inspector has just called in to have some tea. We were talking about our Kirsty.'

'Hasn't she put up with enough from your lot?' he rasped. 'Go away and leave us alone.' He led her away, back into the kitchen.

Jack felt any more intrusion would make things worse, so he went back through the gate and was walking towards his car when Ted thundered up on his tractor.

He turned the engine off and climbed down. 'Inspector, why are you here? I don't suppose you've got any news?'

'No, I'm sorry. I came to apologize for the stress that you and Mary suffered as a result of that unauthorized news broadcast and then the discovery that it wasn't Kirsty after all.'

Ted shook his head. 'If anything, it's made Mary worse. Now she's convinced Kirsty's still alive and is on her way home. It doesn't matter what I say, she won't listen.'

'Josh seems very concerned for her. Does he work on the farm?'

'Yes, he's a good lad. He's taken on a lot to help us over the last couple of years, as well as his job at the youth project. I've got over a hundred acres of land to manage and he looks after Long Ground and Little Bloomer entirely on his own. They're the fields furthest away from the house. He does it all — ploughing, muck-spreading, planting, hedging, ditching — everything. It means I can stay close to the house, milk the cows and keep an eye on Mary. You'd think a young lad would have found himself another girl after all this time, but no — he's stayed faithful to our Kirsty.'

'Right, well I won't keep you. I'm . . . er . . . very sorry.' Jack drove back to the station feeling more concerned than he had for some time. His off-centre nose told him that something wasn't right, but there would be no more jumping to conclusions.

CHAPTER TWENTY-ONE

Since the last WAWA meeting, a lot had been added to the whiteboard and even more had been erased. There was no longer any doubt that Felix Barrington had murdered a young French sex worker and hidden her body, nor that he had ended the lives of Allegra Parnell and Brian Roberts with a shotgun to avoid exposure and punishment. The team was now focused on the death of the man himself, or rather, the manner of it. Jack knew that the coroner would bring a verdict of suicide if the evidence supported it. He picked up a pen and began to make notes on the board.

'There's still a question mark over Zizi Starr's involvement in all this, in light of her claim that Allegra's death was due to her "greed and stupidity". We've heard her explanation about what she meant by that, but it didn't ring true to any of us. It sounded to me like she made it up on the spur of the moment when Gemma surprised her with it. And the whereabouts of Kirsty Jackson are still unknown, although that is still an open MISPER case.'

'Sir, I know it isn't normally within the remit of the MIT to investigate missing persons, but I have some information that might be relevant.' DC Dinkley stood up. 'I went to the Richington Youth Project to see if Roger Goodman remembered Celine Dubois ever going there. He didn't. But on my way out, a couple of girls asked if I was investigating Kirsty's disappearance. It turns out that contrary to Josh Barker's version of events, he and Kirsty were definitely not love's young dream and she was about to dump him. They argued a lot about her ambitions for the future because it wasn't what he had planned for her at all.'

'That's completely different from what he said on the TV appeal, sir.' Clive dredged up the recording from two years ago and played it to them. They listened with interest as a tearful Josh begged whoever was holding "his" Kirsty to let her go. They loved each other, he said, and were planning a life together.

'Do you think we have grounds to pull him in and interview him again, sir?' asked Velma.

Jack was thinking about his recent conversation with Ted Jackson — how Josh had stayed faithful to Kirsty despite her absence and helped out on the farm. The murder of Celine had brought Kirsty's disappearance back under the magnifying glass, and Jack was starting to have some doubts.

'Velma, Aled, did either of you have any plans for this evening? No? Good.' He answered his own question before they could reply. 'Here's what I want you to do. Clive will print off a plan of the Jacksons' farm. Can you do that, Clive?'

'Yep, no problem. I'll get it from the deeds.'

'Velma and Aled, I need you to go for a country stroll past the Jacksons' farm, and accidentally stray from the public footpath into the fields at the top end, furthest away from the house. They're named "Long Ground" and "Little Bloomer". The fields all have a name. It's a tradition that's dying out, now, but Ted Jackson still follows it, as I imagine did his father and grandfather. Because of Mary Jackson's fragile state of mind, I don't want to do anything to upset her further unless I absolutely have to.'

'OK, sir. What are we looking for?' Velma was making notes.

'To be honest, I'm not sure. It's just that your conversation with the two girls has added weight to a nagging doubt that's been going around in my head. Just have a ramble through the fields and see if anything unusual hits you.'

'OK, sir, we've got it.' Aled hoped that if anything did hit them, it wouldn't come from Ted Jackson's shotgun.

After the meeting, as everyone dispersed, Bugsy muttered to Jack, 'Is it the old "nose" again, guv?'

'That's right. Something's making it twitch and if I'm right, I fear we may soon have another body to deal with.'

* * *

'You can see why this is called Long Ground,' said Aled. 'It's narrow at the top and bottom but bloody miles down the sides.' They had walked the entire perimeter.

'I think that might be a slight exaggeration, but I can see what you mean.' Velma stopped and looked down at his trainers. 'I think you may have trodden in something.'

'Damn!' exclaimed Aled. 'Flipping cows. These trainers were new and they cost a fortune.'

Velma reached into her backpack and gave him a handful of tissues. 'To be fair, it's the cows who live here. We're the interlopers.'

Aled wiped off the worst of the cowpat. 'I don't know about you, but I haven't seen anything that doesn't belong in a field on a farm.'

'No, me neither. Let's take a look at the other one. What's it called? Oh yes, Little Bloomer. I wonder why the boss chose those two fields in particular.'

'Dunno but he sometimes follows a hunch,' said Aled. 'I guess you'd know all about hunches, having a psychology degree.'

Velma nodded. 'Believe it or not, researchers have found a way to measure intuition — which is basically what hunches are. It's a brain process that gives people the ability to make decisions without using lengthy analytical reasoning. It relies on a kind of mental blueprint-matching. What the inspector's mind does is trawl through the experiences stored in his long-term memory for similar situations, then makes an ad hoc judgement based on them. It's an unconscious process. The only problem is that intuition isn't very good at picking up flaws in the evidence. Sometimes, the world conspires against us and presents information that's unreliable and misleading. Then, of course, you can get things badly wrong, like when we all believed the body in the Kings Copse was Kirsty Jackson.'

'I can identify with getting things badly wrong. It's what we normal human beings call "Sod's Law", and I reckon that's what's happening here. We've been all around this field as well as Long Ground, and there's nothing to see.'

'Except that tree.' Velma pointed at the only tree in an otherwise treeless field. 'Does that look out of place to you?'

Aled looked. 'Not really. We're in a field. It's full of hedges and grass and green, country-type stuff. Why would a tree be out of place? I was brought up in a little Welsh town with one main street on a steep hill. You climbed up it to get to school in the morning and sprinted back home in the afternoon. Now, a tree would have been well out of place there.'

They walked across and looked at it. 'It's a rowan tree,' said Velma. 'Druids believed it protected the spirits of the dead.' She picked off a berry. 'Look, there's a tiny five-pointed star opposite the stalk. It's a pentagram, an ancient protective symbol. The rowan is considered to be a portal tree, a gateway between this world and another world, an entry and an exit, a kind of threshold that allows you to go somewhere and leave somewhere.'

Aled had unpleasant memories of pentagrams and what he regarded as 'all that black art malarkey', having come close to being sacrificed by a nutter on the tomb of Saint Columbanus in the line of duty. It had been a very scary experience and he had no wish to be reminded of it. 'Velma, you're a very smart lady and a bloody good police officer, and I'm very grateful to you for cutting me down when I was nearly hanging from that tree. But I have to say — you don't half freak me out, sometimes. Come on, let's have a drink in the Richington Arms.'

Velma grinned. 'OK.' She took a few photos on her phone and they went back out of the field to the footpath.

* * *

At the same time that Aled and Velma were drinking warm beer in the Richington Arms, Detective Chief Superintendent Garwood and his wife were in the bar of Kings Richington Golf Club, sipping a gin and tonic with ice and a slice of wizened, preserved lemon from a jar.

'George, are you sure you want to have dinner here?' asked Cynthia. 'Corrie says she's seen a van delivering ready meals at the back door.'

He picked up a menu. 'It says here that all meals are prepared by hand.'

'They are. They use their hands to shove them into the microwave, then they use them again to slide the food out onto a plate.'

'What about the bit that says, "served with fresh, home-grown accompaniments"?'

'They throw on a sprig of parsley. It's growing in a tub in the car park. If you'd said you wanted to eat out, I'd have booked a table at Carlene's bistro. We'd have had a delicious meal, expertly cooked and perfectly served. Or I could have asked Corrie to deliver something.' Cynthia didn't suggest she could have prepared something herself at home because she'd never cooked a meal in her life. It was one of the advantages of having a best friend who was a top-class caterer. What, she argued, was the point of buying fresh ingredients from a food hall only to find you had to fiddle with them when you got them home? 'Why are we really here, George?'

He blustered about getting them seated in the dining room, asking for the wine list and fidgeting with his napkin in an attempt to distract her, knowing she wouldn't approve of the answer. 'What wine would you like, dear?'

Cynthia hadn't been married for over twenty-five years without knowing when her husband was up to something. 'George, why are we here?'

He capitulated. He leaned across and whispered in her ear. 'It's to do with my knighthood.'

'Knighthood!' she squealed. 'Do you mean I'm going to be Lady Cynthia Garwood? Wait till I tell Corrie and Carlene and the rest of the girls in the gang.'

'Keep your voice down!' George looked around, furtively, to see if anyone had heard. 'You mustn't tell anyone. There have been a few setbacks.'

'What sort of setbacks? What has it to do with us coming here?' The waiter arrived then to take their order and she was temporarily diverted. 'I'll have the fillet of wild Scottish salmon, pan-fried without the lemon sauce. And I'd like the side of baby vegetables — just the new potatoes, green beans, some peas and maybe a few spears of asparagus, but without the parsnips, carrots and sweetcorn.' She handed him back the menu.

The waiter looked doubtful. He'd had to deal with her type before. 'I'm afraid the salmon comes poached *in* the lemon sauce, madam, so it isn't possible to serve it without. We don't have any asparagus until the truck arrives from Peru, and the baby vegetables come already cooked and combined in a bowl, so perhaps madam could just pick out the ones she wants to eat and leave the rest?'

George ordered steak and kidney pudding, which the waiter said could take a while. Cynthia imagined it came in a tin so had to be boiled in a saucepan on the hob instead of microwaved. She called after the waiter. 'Don't bother with the garnish of lead-infused parsley, I'll manage without.' She poured herself a generous glass of the house Chardonnay, took a gulp and made a face. 'OK, George, what's so important that we have to sit here eating and drinking overpriced, substandard garbage?'

'After years of prompting, I'd finally persuaded Sir Barnaby to recommend me for a knighthood. He was supposed to provide the Cabinet Office with all the relevant details of my achievements, plus a minimum of two letters of support for the nomination.'

'But George, most of your achievements are down to Jack Dawes and his team. Shouldn't he be the one getting the nomination?'

Garwood snorted. 'Don't be ridiculous, Cynthia. Whoever heard of an iconoclastic, subversive, ignore-the-rules inspector being recommended for a knighthood?'

'I bet I could think of a few. What about that chap from Traffic who reversed the right of way on all the roundabouts on the bypass? After they'd sorted out the accidents, they said it was an inspired piece of civil engineering.'

He cut her off. 'Never mind him. The point is that one of my letters of support was from Felix Barrington. Support from a disgraced magistrate who turned out to be a sexual predator and a triple murderer and who hanged himself is hardly a recommendation, is it?'

'No, I guess not,' Cynthia conceded. 'So why are we here?'

'That chap on the next table — no, don't look round! — is the owner of this and several other golf courses in the county. He comes from a wealthy family and I've been cultivating his friendship. A recommendation from him would be perfect.'

'While you've been doing all this obsequious brown-nosing, have you given a thought to how poor Mallory Barrington is coping with all the adverse gossip? She desperately wants his body released by the coroner, so that she can cremate the bastard and get on with her life.'

'All right, I'll speak to Dawes.' He smiled and nodded as the man on the next table got up to leave with his associates. George stood too. 'I think I'll go and have a quick word with Sir Crispin, just out of courtesy.'

Cynthia shrugged and beckoned to the wine waiter. 'Can you bring me a bottle of something drinkable, please?'

'Of course, madam. How about this to complement the salmon?' He pointed to a Premier Cru Chablis priced at more than twice her entire meal.

Cynthia thought she'd earned it. 'Yes, that will do nicely. Put it on my husband's tab.'

CHAPTER TWENTY-TWO

Velma had printed out the photo of the rowan tree and pinned it to the whiteboard under the image of Kirsty Jackson.

'That was the only thing we spotted that looked unusual, sir.'

Jack examined it closely. 'I agree, Velma, it does look a little out of place in the field. Especially as all the other trees on the farm appear to have been planted as shelter for crops and animals.'

'It looks more decorative than functional,' agreed Gemma.

'Tell the boss what you said about the Druids, Velma,' said Aled. 'It freaked me out.'

'I don't know why,' said Velma. 'Druids can trace their origins to ancient Wales where the order began, long before they began writing about it. You're more than likely descended from one.'

'No, I mean the bit about the rowan being a portal between this world and . . . er . . . other worlds.'

'Is that why you see them in cemeteries?' asked Bugsy.

'Weren't there rowan trees in the forest of Fangorn, where Quickbeam lived?' asked Clive.

Bugsy reckoned no one but Clive would have thought of that. No one but Clive understood it. Jack was thinking hard, saying nothing.

Aled nudged Velma. 'I think the boss is doing that thing — what did you call it? Mental blueprint-matching.'

'OK, team,' Jack said. 'This is what we're going to do. We're going to apply for a search warrant for the Jacksons' farm.'

'Blimey, guv, are you sure?' asked Bugsy.

'Sir, I've read the original MISPER report,' said Clive. 'Uniform searched the farm when the girl first disappeared. It's standard practice. They virtually took the farmhouse apart, combed all the outhouses, the milking parlour, the slurry pit — they even emptied the silage out of the silos. They didn't find any trace.'

'I know, Clive. They were very thorough. But what they didn't do was dig up the fields. There was no indication that it was necessary and it would have been a massive job. But that's what we're going to do now, starting with the one where the rowan tree's growing — Little Bloomer. If my hunch is right, we won't need to dig up the others.'

* * *

When the police convoy arrived outside the Jacksons' farm, Ted was milking and Mary was baking. When Jack and Bugsy knocked on the kitchen door, she hurried to let them in.

'Have you found her? Is Kirsty coming home? I'm baking her favourites, chocolate brownies, because I need to have something nice ready for her.'

Jack couldn't see any point in showing her the search warrant. She was too distracted to understand what it was all about. 'We just need to have a look around your fields, Mrs Jackson. Nothing for you to worry about.'

She flipped a strand of hair out of her eyes with a floury hand. 'Oh. I see. Yes, all right. I'll have warm brownies and a cup of tea ready by the time you come back.'

'Poor soul,' said Bugsy when they were outside. 'Do you reckon we're going to find Kirsty this time, guv?'

'I'm very much afraid we are, Bugsy.'

'A hunch?'

'More of an educated guess. Ted Jackson was extolling Josh's virtues, saying how much he'd helped on the farm since Kirsty disappeared, particularly in the fields furthest away from the house. It meant Ted was always close at hand to look after Mary when she had one of her bad turns. Add to that what Velma found out about Kirsty not seeing eye to eye with Josh about their future – how she planned to dump him for a musical career in London – and you have a pretty suspect situation.'

Bugsy nodded. 'And then they found the rowan tree.'

Police with spades had reached Little Bloomer and looked to Jack for instructions. 'Start just under that tree, please, gentlemen. Then work outwards.' Jack and Bugsy stood a little way off, waiting. The atmosphere was solemn. No conversations, just the sound of spades turning over earth. The officers knew what they had been sent there to find.

It wasn't long before there was a shout and one of the men raised a hand. 'Over here, sir.' They had partially unearthed what was clearly a human body, small and mostly skeletal.

While Jack and Bugsy were looking down at what they'd found, a quad bike roared up behind them.

'Stop! Stop it! You can't do that!' Josh jumped off the bike and ran at the officer, trying to wrestle the spade out of his hand. He was completely out of control, shouting and swearing. 'Leave her alone. She belongs here — with me!'

A couple of the uniformed officers restrained him, as he struggled and choked with rage. 'You've no right! Get off me, you pigs!'

One of the constables produced handcuffs and they looked to Jack for orders.

'Bugsy, caution and arrest Mr Barker on suspicion of murder and unlawful disposal of a dead body, then take him down to the station. Get the duty doctor to look at him.' Josh was hyperventilating with temper and Jack didn't want any accusations of rough handling. 'I'll call Dr Hardacre and the SOCO team. We need the area taped off. This time, I believe we've found Kirsty Jackson.'

* * *

Jack realized he would have to break it to the Jacksons immediately, before some half-baked, self-seeking journalist got in on the act, like the last time.

The parents' reactions were strangely different.

'You think Josh killed our Kirsty and buried her in Little Bloomer?' Ted was dazed with disbelief. 'That can't be. The lad adored her. And even if he did, how could he have kept it secret all this time, with her mother in such a state, believing she was still alive? No, it must have been someone else.'

'We don't know the full facts yet, sir, but Josh is a person of interest and he's helping us with our inquiries. We'll let you know as soon as we have more information.' He hesitated. 'How long has the rowan tree been in that field, Mr Jackson?'

'Since Kirsty's dog died. Must be a good ten years now. We buried Toby there and Kirsty helped to plant the rowan. She was only little, said it had magical powers, like the fairies, and it would protect him. She was caring like that.' He broke down, unable to say any more.

Bugsy wasn't sure Mary Jackson had taken in much of what he'd told her. Her understanding of the news seemed blurred around the edges, as if she was seeing the world through a bewildering fog. 'So you say my Kirsty has been at home, all this time? She didn't go anywhere? She was lying down in Little Bloomer?'

'Something like that, Mrs Jackson,' Bugsy replied. He was far from sure that she realized her daughter was dead.

'It's all over now, Mary,' said Ted, through his tears. He put his arms around her. 'You can stop listening for her key in the door.'

* * *

Big Ron and her team had done their work and the body had been removed. Jack didn't think there would be too many surprises at the post-mortem but it was doubly gut-wrenching, coming so soon after the last young body laid out on the examination table.

Dr Hardacre began positively. 'It's definitely Kirsty Jackson and she's been dead between eighteen months and two and a half years.'

'So she was killed around the same time as the young French girl,' observed Bugsy.

'I haven't said she was killed, Sergeant. That will be for you and the coroner to decide. It's my job to tell you how she died. And apart from the comparable ages of the cadavers, there are very few similarities. This girl was well-nourished, no signs of disease or deficiencies, nothing in the tox report and definitely not pregnant.'

'So, apart from the fact that she's dead, you could say she was pretty healthy?' asked Bugsy.

Big Ron gave him a scathing look. 'With your gallows humour, Sergeant Malone, I expect you probably would say that, but *I* wouldn't. Once again, decomposition was well advanced due to exposure to the elements. I'm surprised that given the situation of the corpse in a farm field, it hadn't been disturbed by animals. Often foxes dig up a bone or two and make off with it. Unlike the other burial in that ghastly copse, this grave appeared to have been looked after.'

'Cause of death, Doc?' asked Bugsy.

'Blunt force trauma to the back of the head. On impact, a piece of bone broke loose from the skull and was forced into the cranium, with concentric fractures forming around the break area. Just the one blow, but death would have been instantaneous.'

'Can you tell us what she was hit with, Dr Hardacre?' Jack asked.

She frowned. 'I can make a guess. The bone fragment often takes on the approximate shape of the object that caused it. Given the samples I took, I'd say it was a rock of the type local to the area. What I can't be sure of is whether the rock hit her, or she hit the rock.'

'You mean she could have fallen on it?'

'It's possible. After this length of time, it's hard to be definite, and before you ask, it's highly unlikely that the rock is still around, let alone identifiable.' She looked across at Jack. 'I understand you have a suspect in custody?'

'Yes, Doctor. But we haven't charged him yet.'

'Well, I suggest you nail this one before he has a chance to hang himself.'

* * *

Far from appearing suicidal, Josh Barker was in deep conversation with the duty solicitor. He was no longer foaming at the mouth with rage, but appeared to be speaking rationally. They stopped when Jack and Bugsy entered the room with Gemma, who was there to work the digital recorder. They went through the protocols of who was present.

'Before you start questioning my client,' said the solicitor, 'he wishes to change the statement that he made two years ago, at the time of Miss Jackson's disappearance.' He looked encouragingly at Josh who began, hesitantly.

'It was an accident. It wasn't my fault.'

'Just tell us what happened in your own words, Mr Barker,' invited Jack.

He moistened his lips. 'We'd been to a dance at the youth project. We left about nine o'clock and I was driving her home when she suddenly said she felt sick and would I stop the car. I'd only just bought it and she hadn't ridden in it before. Anyway, I stopped at the crossroads and she got out, saying she'd walk the rest of the way to get some fresh air. That much is still true. She started walking down the road to the farm when I saw her in my headlights suddenly trip and fall over backwards. I got out of the car and ran to help her. She must have hit her head on something because there was all this blood. I tried to bring her round but she wasn't breathing.'

'Why didn't you call an ambulance? You must have had your phone.'

He glanced at the solicitor. 'The battery was flat.'

'What about Kirsty's phone?' pressed Jack. 'Was that flat, too?'

'I don't know. I just panicked. I picked her up and put her in the back of the car and drove her home.'

'Is that your new statement?' asked Bugsy, in disbelief.

'Yes.'

'But she never reached home, did she?'

Barker looked at his brief, who nodded for him to continue. 'Er . . . no. When we got home, I parked at the end of the farm, by the fields, to check on her before her mum saw her. She still wasn't breathing and I realized she was dead.'

'Then what?'

'Well, we were right next to the perimeter fence, so I carried her into Little Bloomer and buried her under the rowan tree. I knew she'd like it there next to Toby, her dead dog.'

Jack took a deep breath. 'Josh, I realize you've spent most of your life working on a farm, but you weren't living in a vacuum. You must know something about correct procedures. You can't just bury a body without telling anyone. It's against the law.'

'It would have been dark. How could you see what you were doing?' asked Bugsy.

'She was mine!' He was starting to get agitated again. 'We were going to get married. I wasn't going to let anyone else mess around with her, was I?'

The solicitor could see things were beginning to unravel. 'I think my client needs a break and some refreshment, Inspector.' He stood up indicating that Josh wouldn't be answering any further questions until he'd had a chance to calm him down and give him instructions.

Gemma said out loud who was leaving the room and turned off the recorder. They took the opportunity to have some refreshment themselves back in the incident room.

'Where did he get a spade to dig the grave?' insisted Gemma.

'Good point. It's not the sort of thing you'd take to a dance, is it?' said Bugsy.

'Especially not in a Mini.' Gemma's face bore an expression that said, 'I don't believe a word of it'. 'What about the blood? Big Ron reckoned there would have been a lot of it from a head wound like that. Why wasn't it found at the time?'

Clive had pulled up the MISPER report again. 'Obviously they drove all around the crossroads looking for her, but there's no mention of any blood. It wouldn't have been a full fingertip forensics search because at that time, there was no reason to believe she was dead, just disappeared on the walk home. It was assumed she'd been abducted.'

'So, did chummy go back afterwards and clean it up?' asked Mitch.

'What if he picked up a rock and whacked her with it while she was still inside the car?' suggested Aled. 'The blood would have been a bugger to clean off but not impossible. I remember when I had a full-on nosebleed in my car, it went all over the—'

'Aled, son, I'm trying to eat a jam doughnut, here,' complained Bugsy.

'Does anyone else think Josh Barker may not be telling us the whole truth?' asked Jack.

'Too many discrepancies in his statement,' agreed Gemma. 'His brief is clearly going for accidental death. We need the CPS to charge him with murder or the worst he'll cop for is concealment, unlawful disposal of a body, withholding evidence and maybe perverting the course of justice. He'll turn up in court in a suit, short hair, a scrubbed, innocent, twelve-year-old-looking face and shed a few tears while giving his evidence. A sympathetic jury will accept his sob story that he was traumatized at losing his childhood sweetheart and wasn't thinking clearly and by the time he realized what he'd done was wrong, he was too scared to go back and change his story.'

'If they refer him for a psychiatric report, he could get away with it altogether, just a few months in hospital having therapy,' added Velma. 'A good psychotherapist could even have him declared unfit to plead due to PTSD caused by the incident.'

'I don't think we should let that happen, especially after he's allowed Mary Jackson to go on believing her daughter might still be alive for the last two years,' declared Gemma. 'He actually sat next to her on the TV appeal, snivelling and begging whoever was holding "his" Kirsty to let her go, when he knew exactly where she was, the duplicitous little weasel. I could wring his neck.'

'Any suggestions as to what line our interrogation should take, apart from neck-wringing?' asked Jack.

'Never mind psychotherapy, I think we should let Gemma slap him around a bit until he tells the truth,' said Aled.

'I hope you're joking, son,' said Bugsy, half-inclined to agree.

'Of course I am, Sarge. But we can't let him get away with it.'

'Has anybody been in touch with Barker's parents to tell them what's going on?' It suddenly occurred to Jack that Josh hadn't asked for a phone call, but at nineteen, he hadn't needed a member of his family present.

'I have, sir,' said Mitch. 'Apparently it's an important day in the Church calendar. His father's a lay preacher and his mother's a churchwarden and they're both heavily involved in the service preparations. His father said it was most inconvenient as he had a sermon to write. Josh is an adult now, and they would only come if it was absolutely necessary.'

Jack wondered how necessary they would consider it if their son turned out to be looking at a murder charge. He glanced at his watch. 'He's had long enough to make up his story. Let's take it apart.'

CHAPTER TWENTY-THREE

Back in the interview room, the digital recorder was set up once again and Josh looked calm and self-confident. He sat smiling pleasantly, his hands in his lap. His solicitor had told him he was, on no account, to lose his temper or say anything incautious. If he was in any doubt about a question, he should look to him for advice.

Jack began. 'Mr Barker, there are just one or two points in your account of events that I should like to clarify. You say that after Kirsty fell and hit her head, you drove her dead body to Little Bloomer and buried her.'

'Yeah. I knew she'd be safe there and I could look after her.'

'Where did you get the spade?' It was a simple, blunt question and Bugsy watched him for a response. He was certainly crafty, this lad, but not very bright.

'What?' Barker stopped smiling. 'I don't understand. What spade?'

'The one you used to dig Kirsty's grave. You must have used a spade.'

'Oh. I see.' He thought for a bit. 'I borrowed one off the farm.'

'Let me get this absolutely straight, Josh,' said Jack. You drove Kirsty's body to the lane at the far end of the fields, then walked back to the farm to get a spade and then back to Little Bloomer and buried her. How long did it take you?'

'Er . . . I can't remember. A long time, I suppose.'

Jack looked at Bugsy and he took over. 'You left the dance about nine o'clock, so it would have been dark.'

'Yeah, I suppose it would.'

'Did you see Ted or Mary Jackson when you went to fetch the spade?'

His calm facade was cracking. 'No, I never saw nobody. They'd have gone to bed.'

'But you could see well enough to find the rowan tree and dig the grave?'

Josh looked at his solicitor, whose face was blank. 'No, you've got it all wrong. It wasn't dark when I buried her, it was daylight.'

'I'm sorry, Mr Barker. I don't understand.'

'I never said I buried her the same night she had her accident. It was the next day.'

'That isn't what you told us a moment ago.' Bugsy and Jack exchanged glances.

'You confused me. You're twisting my words to make me look guilty of something. It's what you people do.'

'What did you do with Kirsty's body between putting her in your car that night and burying her next day?' asked Bugsy.

The horrified expression on the solicitor's face indicated that this was the first he'd heard of it.

'I left her in my car. I drove home, put it in the garage and went to bed. Then I went back early next morning to get the spade and bury her. Don't you understand anything?'

The solicitor put a restraining hand on his arm but it didn't work.

'Well, I'm sorry, Mr Barker, but it's hard to keep up when you keep changing your story,' said Bugsy. 'Didn't it occur to you at that point that you should tell somebody — like her parents?'

'No, it bloody well didn't!' He stood up and pushed back his chair with such force that it nearly tipped over. The uniformed constable guarding the door stepped forward to restrain him but Jack waved him away.

'Please sit down, Josh, we need to get to the bottom of this. There's obviously something you're not telling us.'

He sat down again and glowered at Gemma, who hadn't spoken. 'What are you looking at? Kirsty used to look at me like that — like you think you're so smart and I'm stupid, but it didn't work, did it?'

'Why don't you start again, son?' Bugsy poured him a glass of water. 'Tell us exactly what happened between you and Kirsty that night.'

'I really don't think that's a good idea,' said the solicitor, anxiously. 'I need a break to give my client further advice.'

'No!' shouted Josh. 'I've had enough of this. It's time people knew the truth about dear, perfect little Kirsty and her big ideas.' He gulped some water. 'We were at the dance, having a good time, or so I thought. Then come about half past eight, she ups and says she wants to go home. She needs an early night before some sort of stupid music exam, next day.'

'So, what did you say?' asked Bugsy.

'I said I wanted to stay, so she said she'd ring her dad to come and fetch her. Well, I told her not to bother and I'd drive her. Halfway home, she drops the bombshell, doesn't she?'

'What bombshell would that be, Josh?' *Here it comes*, thought Jack. *The reason for all the rows that the girls told Velma about.*

'She says she's sorry, but she doesn't want to see me anymore. She was going to move on with her life and she thought I should, too. I ask you — how would you have felt? We'd been together since primary school and she thought she could end it, just like that.'

'Did you ask her why?' asked Jack.

'Course I did. She said she didn't want to get married, live on the farm and have my kids. She wanted a career

177

playing the piano. That bloke, the one who got shot, he'd filled her head with daft ideas. Told her she could be a concert pianist one day. Play all over the world, he said. What sort of life is that for a woman?'

'A very good one, if she was talented enough,' said Jack.

'No, not for my Kirsty. She belonged at home as my wife, looking after me. It's what we always planned, right from when we were kids.'

'You might have, Josh, but she grew up and wanted a different life.' Bugsy could see he was getting more and more truculent. Soon, he'd tell them what he did out of sheer petulance.

'Yeah, well I soon put a stop to that nonsense, didn't I? I couldn't have her running free, mixing with other blokes. I'm not stupid. I know where that would have ended.'

'So what happened when you told her that?' Everyone held their breath, except the solicitor, who was opening and closing his mouth like a goldfish, but not actually saying anything.

'She told me to stop the car and we both got out. We stood at the crossroads arguing. She wouldn't see my point of view, wouldn't accept that I knew what was best for her. In the end, she said she'd had enough of my old-fashioned ideas, she didn't want to discuss it anymore and she'd walk the rest of the way home. She leaned inside the car to get her handbag, so I picked up a rock and hit her on the back of the head with it.'

'What did you do with the rock, Mr Barker?'

'Well, it was all covered in her blood, so I didn't think I'd leave it there, in case some busybody found it. I took it with me and buried it with her.'

Jack looked across at Bugsy and nodded. 'Stand up, Mr Barker. I'm charging you with the murder of Kirsty Jackson. You do not have to say anything, but—'

His face was distorted with anger and frustration. 'No, listen to me, you've got it all wrong. It wasn't murder. It was for her own good. I didn't have a choice. I was protecting her. God knows what would have happened to her if I'd let her go away to London. And what about me? Surely I deserved some consideration?'

They cuffed him and took him away to be processed.

* * *

Back in the incident room, Aled had made tea. They all needed one — a strong one, and chocolate biscuits.

'Gemma, I reckon you need to make an appointment with your dentist,' said Bugsy.

'Why, Sarge?'

'Because I could hear you grinding your teeth right across the room. You must have a mouthful of crumbling molars by now.'

She pulled a face. 'I really can't believe that in the twenty-first century, there are still blokes like Barker. The whole idea of the "little woman" chained to the sink doing her husband's bidding in return for being kept died out decades ago, together with corsets, spitfires and unavoidable pregnancies. He's living in a time warp.'

'It's gender stereotyping,' said Velma. 'Women are meant to be nurturing and avoid dominance and men are supposed to be assertive and avoid weakness. Believe it or not, studies have shown that the concept is still quite common in some unenlightened communities. For example, there are men out there who believe women can't drive as well as men, simply because they're women. They think it's some kind of congenital defect.'

'Well, how stupid is that?' Gemma turned on Aled, her cheerful whipping boy in all things gender-controversial. 'How many accidents have you had?'

He paused, halfway from dipping a biscuit in his tea. 'Dunno. Half a dozen or so, I guess.'

'Did you pass the police driving test?'

'Eventually.'

'There you are, you see. I passed first time and I've only ever had one accident. It was a bloody big one, admittedly. I totalled an ice cream van, but it was the only one.'

'In Barker's defence, the psychologist's approach would take into account that he has very conformist, authoritative parents,' said Velma. 'Added to which, he will have observed the Jacksons in a very traditional marriage that appeared to be happy. He's grown up in this stifled environment, thinking that domination is the only way a relationship should work.' She filched the last chocolate digestive from under Aled's nose. 'On the other hand, psychology isn't a cop-out for criminals. It could simply be that he's a selfish, pig-headed, chauvinist bully, determined to get his own way at all costs — even if that meant murder.'

'Not unlike Felix Barrington,' said Jack.

'Exactly like Barrington, sir, but he'd had years of practice. The irony is that Roger Goodman told me the aim of the youth project was to help young people develop healthy relationships and make decisions that are right for them, not manipulate them into preconceived and outdated activities. It didn't have any effect on Josh, did it?'

* * *

Corrie was shocked. She had taken a rare break from catering to enjoy coffee and a slice of Charlotte Russe with Cynthia Garwood at a table in the window of Chez Carlene. As usual, news had travelled fast. The *Richington Echo* had devoted the entire front page to the arrest and subsequent murder charge of Josh Barker. They had trawled the archives for a picture of him, seventeen years old, making his tearful media appeal for someone to find sweet-sixteen Kirsty, his 'only love'. The headline read: *Teen killer of budding concert pianist finally unmasked after two years.*

'Poor Mary Jackson.' Corrie wiped cream off her chin with one of the posh napkins that Carlene had recently acquired, embellished with the name of the bistro and a discreet Michelin star.

'That boy was like a son to the Jacksons,' asserted Cynthia. 'Can you imagine — two years of working for them, grieving with them, eating breakfasts in their kitchen, when all the time he knew he'd killed their daughter and buried her in one of their fields? How evil is that?'

'About as evil as Felix Barrington, I guess, except he's dead. Josh Barker will get all kinds of counselling and reports on his state of mind. Jack says the CPS is going for a murder charge but may have to amend it to unlawful act manslaughter, as they can't prove premeditation. His brief is claiming he lashed out on the spur of the moment — a crime of passion, because he couldn't bear to lose her. He's playing the "diminished responsibility" card and all that pseudo-justification that defence barristers resort to when they want to make a name for themselves.'

Cynthia sniffed. 'That doesn't explain why he kept it quiet all this time, does it? I wonder what his holier-than-thou parents are making of it. They never did approve of Kirsty, especially when they found out she was planning a career as a professional pianist. You'd have thought she intended to play naked in the window of Richington Department Store or bash out a few tunes on the honky-tonk down the Richington Arms.'

'According to the *Echo*, when asked for a comment, Mr and Mrs Barker said they were "praying for their son's soul".'

'It's a bit late for that. They should have brought him up with more respect for the earthly body, never mind the immortal soul.' Cynthia poured them more coffee from the cafetière. 'Have you seen Mallory Barrington lately? I'm worried about her. She's missed several meetings of the youth project charity committee and the fundraiser is coming up soon.'

'Give her a chance,' said Corrie. 'Once she's finally cremated the miserable old scrote that she was obliged to call a husband for twenty years, I'm sure she'll be back in circulation.'

* * *

As it turned out, events moved rather faster than expected. The coroner, having taken into account everything that had emerged at the inquest, determined that Barrington's death was caused by suicide. Jack gave the team the news.

'Despite the intrepid reconstruction by Aled and the cerebral assessment from Velma, both casting doubt on Barrington's suicide, we must be aware that the standard of proof — by that I mean the level of evidence needed by coroners to conclude whether a death was caused by suicide — has been lowered from the criminal standard of "beyond all reasonable doubt" to the civil standard of "on the balance of probabilities". On that basis, I think we're all agreed that while there may have been reasonable doubt, the balance of probabilities points to suicide. It means that Mallory Barrington can have her husband cremated and get on with her life, and we can draw a line under this case and move on. All in favour say, "Aye."'

'Aye' they chorused.

CHAPTER TWENTY-FOUR

The Richington Youth Project's annual jumble sale had been overwhelmed with contributions from folk eager to get rid of junk that had been cluttering up their homes for years while feeling self-righteous about donating it to a good cause. Long tables laid out in rows lined the crowded community hall, each loaded with items of every kind. Volunteers were sorting through them, attaching prices, and in some cases, pouncing on the best stuff, before the public could get a look-in.

Down at the far end, Mallory Barrington presided over a bric-a-brac stall. Items ranged from the tacky 'Souvenir from Brightsea' egg timers — bought in a moment of holiday hysteria — to some rather nice ceramic figurines. Mallory had herself donated the pretentious collection of crystal glass decanters once owned by her late, unlamented husband. She hated them. Whenever she looked at them, she could see Felix pouring himself a brandy and strutting about in that accursed dressing gown. She had priced them low enough to be sure they would sell, even if bargain hunters only filled them with bath oils instead of brandy and kept them on the bathroom shelf. She rejoiced in the knowledge that Felix would have hated any of his possessions to be used to raise money for charity. He'd believed that charities enabled scroungers and layabouts to take advantage of handouts, instead of working for a living.

Project Leader Roger Goodman walked around the hall smiling and thanking people for their efforts. He was clearly a very popular member of the community, and had the ability to draw people together in a common cause. He paused at the bric-a-brac stall. 'Good morning, Mrs Barrington. How are you?'

She smiled. 'I'm fine, Mr Goodman, thank you.'

'Isn't this a wonderful turnout?'

'Yes, isn't it? People have been so generous.'

He leaned towards her and spoke softly. 'Chin up. Not long now.'

He moved on to the next stall.

* * *

It was usual practice for the volunteers on the clothing stalls to empty the pockets of garments before they were put up for sale. Flora Crumpton was one such person, and she never ceased to be amazed at the things she found. So far she had eight biros, three pocketknives, four pounds and twenty-five pence in coins, and a set of dentures. She had her eye on Felix Barrington's very expensive designer dressing gown. It would make the perfect present for Mr Crumpton's birthday. At the recommended price of twenty pounds, it was a snip from the two thousand that Mrs Barrington said it had cost. As soon as it was decently possible, she grabbed it and put her twenty pounds in the float. Almost as an afterthought, she felt in the pockets and pulled out a handful of tissues scented with gentlemen's cologne, one cashmere sock and a sheet of computer paper folded in four and with typing on it. She unfolded it and read:

I know what you did. I want £5,000 to keep quiet or I go to the police and you go to jail. Wait for instructions about where to leave the money.

Her first instinct was to screw it up and throw it away, but with Mr Barrington dead in what the *Echo* had described as "suspicious circumstances", she thought it might be important. At the same time, she wasn't sure who to hand it to without getting involved in something unpleasant. She put it to one side while she considered what to do.

* * *

Corrie's contribution to the project's funds was to provide the refreshments. Just before the official opening of the community hall doors, she was in the kitchen with Cynthia setting out an array of cakes, biscuits and other tempting fancies. She put Cynthia in charge of the tea urn, as there was little that she could mess up. They were to be joined by more volunteers as soon as the hordes rushed in and demand became overwhelming.

'Did you see the long queue outside when we drove up?' asked Cynthia.

'This is always one of the best attended charity events of the year.' Corrie was putting prices on the various trays of food. 'It's mostly down to Roger. The youth project is lucky to have him. It would be hard to find a replacement if he ever decides to leave.'

'I doubt if he will. He's committed to supporting the young people of Kings Richington and he gets excellent results.' Cynthia frowned. 'Josh Barker let him down badly. Roger took it very hard. It wasn't his fault — that young man had everybody fooled.'

'Jack says his confession and pleading guilty to unlawful act manslaughter will probably go in Josh's favour, but he'll still get a custodial sentence and as he's over eighteen, it'll be in a prison, not a young offenders' institute.'

Someone tapped on the shutter that closed off the kitchen from the main hall. Corrie called out, 'Sorry, we're not open yet.'

'Mrs Dawes?' said a voice. 'It's Flora Crumpton. I wonder if I might have a quick word.'

Corrie opened the door and let her in. 'Hello, Flora. What can I do for you?'

'I saw you come in and I immediately thought you were the right person to speak to, you being married to a police officer.'

Either her cat's gone missing or neighbours are parking in her driveway, guessed Corrie. Those were the most common reasons they wanted Jack's help. The fact that his job was to investigate murders didn't seem to matter. 'How can I help?'

'It's this.' Flora produced the note. 'I found it in the late Mr Barrington's dressing gown pocket. I suppose I could just give it to Mrs Barrington, but as you'll see, it's a bit unpleasant, and she's had a bad time of it lately. I didn't want to upset her over something that might just be kids playing the fool.'

As soon as Corrie read it, she realized the implications. 'Thanks, Flora. You leave it with me and I'll make sure Jack sees it.' As soon as she'd gone, Corrie grabbed a polythene bag from under the counter and slipped the note inside.

'What is it?' asked Cynthia.

'If I'm not much mistaken, it's the reason Felix Barrington shot Allegra Parnell and her husband. I'm going to give it to Jack.' She recalled the conversation she'd had with Jack when she'd suggested that somebody, not necessarily Allegra, might have attempted to blackmail Barrington, and maybe he'd shot the wrong person. 'This note, Cynthia, could be the tin-opener to a very large can of worms.' Corrie looked back at her, fiddling with the tap on the urn. 'How are you doing with the tea? The doors open in ten minutes.'

'I don't think the urn's working. The water's still cold.'

'Have you switched it on at the mains?' asked Corrie.

'Oh. Does it need electricity? You never said.'

* * *

That evening, Jack arrived home only slightly ahead of Corrie. By the time he heard her key in the door, he had taken off his coat and made a pot of tea.

'You were right about there not being many people at Barrington's funeral.' He poured her a cup. 'I thought

Mallory might have been there, if only to watch his coffin go into the furnace so she could be absolutely sure she'd seen the last of him. Not even his cronies from the golf club turned out.'

Corrie sank down in a chair, having been on her feet all day. 'Mallory was at the jumble sale getting rid of all his possessions. I guess that was her idea of closure, and who can blame her? And why would the funny handshake brigade have been there? Certainly not to pay their respects. He was no use to them dead. They only befriended him to get an easy ride if they found themselves up before him in the magistrates' court.'

'Cynical, but I guess you're right. What's for supper? I'm starving.'

'I haven't had time to think about supper, so I booked a table at Chez Carlene. I thought we'd eat there. But first, there's something I need to show you.'

Corrie fetched her handbag and found the plastic bag containing the folded computer paper. She opened it out with the kitchen tweezers that she used to tweak pin bones from salmon. 'Don't touch it — there might be fingerprints.'

Jack read the message. 'Where did you get this?'

'Flora Crumpton found it in the pocket of Barrington's dressing gown at the jumble sale. She brought it straight to me.'

'Did she handle it?'

'I'm afraid so. She didn't know what it was until she pulled it out and read it.'

Jack frowned. 'So Barrington was being blackmailed, like you suspected.'

'I doubt if he ever intended to hand over any money, never mind wait for instructions about where to leave it,' said Corrie. 'Given his temperament and massive sense of entitlement, I imagine he got into a drunken rage, assumed the note was from Allegra, and completely lost control. Then he grabbed his shotgun and drove to Richington Mallet to shut her up. The rest we know.'

'Put it back in the plastic bag. I'll have it checked for fingerprints tomorrow. We'll need to take Mrs Crumpton's, and we've already got Barrington's, so with any luck, any other prints we find on there will belong either to Allegra or the blackmailer.'

'I don't believe it was Allegra. Blackmail wasn't her style. Adultery, yes, but not blackmail. It'll be somebody close to her — somebody she confided in.'

* * *

Chez Carlene was busy, as it was every night of the week. The bistro was on the corner of Richington High Street, with picture windows all around. In the summer, there were tables outside under a striped yellow awning. Inside, it was decorated in Parisian style — strongly influenced by Carlene's French partner, Antoine — so that customers might almost be dining on the Left Bank. By day, it was a brasserie, cool and dark with mottled, sea-green tabletops and French accordion music playing softly in the background. At night, it turned into a sophisticated bistro, stylish and trendy, serving superb food and wine.

Carlene came forward to welcome them and kissed them both on the cheek. 'Hello, Inspector Jack, Mrs D. I've reserved you a table in the window.' Once they were seated, she brought them a carafe of their favourite wine, some olives, crusty French bread and the à la carte menu. 'What can I get you? The cassoulet is particularly popular tonight or there's salmon en papillote if you'd prefer fish.' She bent to whisper in Corrie's ear. 'When you get a chance, have a look at the couple sitting at the table in the alcove.'

They both ordered the cassoulet. After Carlene had gone to get it, Corrie glanced casually over her shoulder at the table set back from the main restaurant and tucked away in the alcove.

'Well, that's a surprise,' she muttered.

'What is?' Jack was dipping some bread in a dish of olive oil and balsamic vinegar.

'Mallory Barrington and Roger Goodman. They're over there having dinner together.'

Jack looked. The couple was deep in earnest conversation and completely oblivious to their surroundings and the other diners. He shrugged. 'What's wrong with that? I expect he's treating her to supper as thanks for helping with the jumble sale.'

Corrie sighed. 'Jack, you're supposed to be a detective.'

'What?' He looked puzzled. 'You said yourself that Mallory hasn't been eating properly. I expect Goodman thought the same. Aren't they on the committees of the same charities or something?'

'Yes, but I think their relationship has developed into rather more than committee colleagues. He's holding her hand under the table.'

'Why not? He's a decent enough bloke. Bugsy and Gemma think he's the bee's knees since he punched Nigel the Knob's lights out for bullying. Mallory's free at last and deserves some happiness after twenty years married to that brute Barrington. It's not like you to be judgemental, sweetheart. I say good luck to them.'

'Yes, you're right. Good luck to them.' If Jack, with his acute policeman's antennae, never mind his twitchy nose, didn't see anything suspicious about their liaison, thought Corrie, then neither would she.

CHAPTER TWENTY-FIVE

Jack gave the note to Forensics first thing next morning, asking for a quick turnaround. Sergeant Parsloe sent a police car to bring in Flora Crumpton to have her fingerprints taken for elimination purposes. It was the high spot of her week. Inquisitive neighbours saw the police car arrive and take Flora away. When she told them why, it became the talking point of the cul-de-sac. It was twenty-four hours before Jack got the final results.

'OK, sir, whose were the prints on the blackmail note?' Aled's pen was poised to write it on the whiteboard.

'I can tell you whose they weren't,' said Jack. 'They weren't Allegra Parnell's.'

'So, even though she had her father's document describing how Barrington had committed rape and murder, she didn't report him to the police or challenge him with it?' Gemma was disappointed. Until now, she'd had a grudging admiration for Allegra Parnell, a successful solicitor who had led a vigorous, abandoned, uncompromising life, with scant regard for the men she had used along the way. Gemma had no problem with that. But to allow a man like Barrington to get away with the murder of a young, defenceless girl was unforgivable.

'Whoever sent that blackmail note was effectively the trigger for Allegra's shooting,' observed Bugsy. 'No pun intended.'

'It was Zizi Starr, wasn't it, sir?' DC Dinkley was confident. 'It explains what Gemma overheard when she drank that final toast to Allegra.'

'Correct, Velma,' said Jack. 'It also explains why she was so scared when she thought Barrington might guess that Allegra had shared the information with her and come to shoot her next.'

'And why she calmed down after we discovered his dead body,' added Gemma.

'Do we pull her in now, guv?' asked Bugsy.

'Oh yes, I think so,' said Jack. 'She has a lot of questions to answer, not least why she didn't tell us she had a pretty good idea it was Barrington who murdered Allegra Parnell and Brian Roberts right at the beginning, when she found their bodies. It might have speeded up the investigation.'

'I guess she'll answer charges of attempted blackmail and withholding evidence, will she, sir?' asked Aled.

'Possibly, Aled, but I don't think we should regard her as public enemy number one. For a start, most of the people involved in this investigation are dead and beyond either retribution or reprisal.'

* * *

In her psychedelic, perfume-filled shop, Zizi Starr was dealing the tarot cards for what must have been the tenth time. Whichever way she cut them, the Three of Swords, representing rejection, sadness, loneliness, heartbreak, separation and grief relentlessly appeared. She missed her friend Allegra more than she could ever have imagined. If only she could turn back the clock.

The door chimes announced the arrival of two uniformed police constables. 'Miss Starr? Would you come with us, please? You're wanted for questioning down at the station.'

This is it, she thought. *Time to confess to my mindless folly.* She wondered what they would charge her with. Strangely, she realized she didn't much care anymore. Wordlessly, she collected her jacket and shoulder bag and went with them.

* * *

Mallory Barrington checked her passport once again and double-checked the paperwork that was needed to take the dogs on the plane and into the United States. All their veterinary health certificates had been completed satisfactorily and they were both chipped. There was no way she would leave her faithful Bilbo and Baggins behind. Without their courageous intervention, she might well be dead instead of Felix.

Roger had organized everything and had assured her that all was in order. Arrangements had been made for the private sale of her house and its contents and both cars, and an offshore account had been set up to deposit the money. Her new life beckoned and she felt a combination of excitement and trepidation.

Throughout their bitter, barren twenty-year marriage, she and Felix had never been abroad because he couldn't see any good reason to travel. In the early days, on the rare occasions she had dared to suggest a holiday abroad, he had asked her to explain the point of tedious flights to filthy countries full of ignorant foreigners and inedible food. She could smile, now, at his absurd, xenophobic views and be thankful she was no longer constrained by them. All that remained was to pack her essentials. She would buy everything else she needed when they arrived in the United States. Their Winnebago camper home would be waiting for them and they were about to embark upon the trip of a lifetime. She could only imagine the disdain and disgust such a project would have provoked in Felix compared to the absolute joy and liberation she was feeling.

Her last task was to write the letter — and she was determined that she *would* write it, despite Roger telling her it was unwise. She would make careful arrangements to ensure it was delivered to DI Dawes, after she and Roger were safely out of the country, on the move and untraceable. She knew that if she didn't unburden her soul, she could never take that final step to freedom.

* * *

'Can I get you a cup of tea, Miss Starr?' Bugsy thought she looked thinner and even more strained than the last time he saw her.

'Do you have chamomile or lavender?'

'I doubt it. I don't think the canteen runs to exotic beverages. It's only tea or coffee, and some days, it's hard to tell one from the other.'

'Then I'll pass, thank you.' She looked around her at the stark, austere interview room. It smelled, inexplicably, of cabbage water, cats' pee and stale sweat. She supposed that she was more aware of bad smells since, in The Galaxy Boutique, she was surrounded every day by fragrant ones.

When she had first arrived at the station, Zizi had contacted Ms Carmichael, a colleague of Allegra's from Parnell & Parnell. The lady in question had arrived with all haste and she and Zizi had been deeply engrossed in conversation for some time before the interview began. They had been shown the blackmail note, told where it had been found and informed that Zizi's fingerprints were on it — fingerprints that had remained on the police database following her charge of dealing in psychoactive substances. She had been brought in to explain why such prints had cropped up on a note demanding money from Felix Telford Barrington.

Velma was in charge of the recorder. At Jack's instigation, she switched it on and made the customary announcements.

'Has my client been charged, Inspector?' asked Ms Carmichael.

'No, but you should be aware that charges may follow after she has made her statement.'

'Ms Starr has opted, against my advice, to provide a full account of her involvement with regard to the deaths of Allegra Parnell and Brian Roberts. I reserve the right to interrupt if I feel she may be incriminating herself unnecessarily. But having heard the facts, I must warn you that I don't believe she has a case to answer.' She looked at Zizi encouragingly.

Zizi sipped some water. 'First, I want to say that Allegra was my dearest friend, and had been since we were small. I would never have knowingly done anything to harm her.' Tears welled up in her eyes and Jack waited until she could continue. 'After Grafton died, she had to take up the reins of the law firm, which, I might add, she was more than capable of doing.'

Ms Carmichael nodded in agreement. Allegra Parnell had been a good boss and an inspired divorce lawyer. Her private life had been unorthodox, to say the least, but she got results, which was what counted if you were to survive in the legal profession.

Zizi sipped more water. 'She'd been looking for some documents relating to the purchase of Oak Lodge for insurance purposes, and since she couldn't find them anywhere else, she thought her father may have locked them in the safe. She knew the combination and opened it. There was one envelope inside, marked "Private and Confidential". She opened it and found what you now know to be Grafton's sworn account, written just before he died of a cardiac arrest. It described what Felix Barrington had told him about raping and strangling a young girl two years ago. It didn't name the victim but Allegra assumed it was Kirsty Jackson. The fact that it turned out to be another sixteen-year-old doesn't make it any less heinous. I knew Allegra's dad well and he was an honourable and principled man. The fact that he didn't immediately come to you with the information Allegra put down to misplaced loyalty to Barrington. She said she guessed her father must have agreed to give him a few days' grace to confess, before he would undoubtedly have turned him in. But poor Grafton died before he could do it.'

'Why didn't Allegra bring the document to the police as soon as she found it?' asked Bugsy. 'As a legal professional, she must have known it was the right thing to do.'

Zizi felt the tears running down her cheeks. 'She wanted to, but I stopped her. It was my fault. I asked her to wait until I'd got some cash out of the evil man to make up for the huge fine he had imposed on me in the magistrate's court. It had practically put me out of business. I know it was wrong but it seemed like the perfect karma. I firmly believe in karma.'

'What exactly is karma?' asked Bugsy, of nobody in particular.

'It's mirrored energy, Sarge,' explained Velma. 'According to the karmic laws of cause and effect, all our actions, thoughts and intentions create energy. If you put out good energy, good things will come back to you and vice versa. Negative energy means bad things will return to you. It's like an echo.'

'Or a boomerang?' suggested Bugsy.

'That's exactly right, officer,' said Zizi, 'and in this case, bad things returned to me. Barrington got my note and believed it had come from Allegra, because she'd found out from her father what he'd done. He went to her house with his shotgun and killed her — and poor Brian too. And it was all my fault.' She began to sob uncontrollably.

'I don't think my client can reasonably be expected to continue without a break, do you, Inspector?' Ms Carmichael stood up, indicating that an interval was required.

* * *

'OK, so what do we think?' Jack was back in the incident room with the team.

'She's confessed to knowing what Barrington said he did, but she had no proof that he actually did it. Even the affidavit wasn't proof because Barrington didn't sign it,' said Clive.

'It was all hearsay,' added Aled. 'She was just chancing her arm.'

'She couldn't have predicted what he would do when he got the blackmail note, despite her self-proclaimed powers of clairvoyance,' said Gemma. 'He might have just ignored it or denied the whole thing — pretended he meant the confession as a joke, albeit a sick one, and he hadn't intended for Parnell to take it seriously. That's what any sane person would have done — blagged his way out, not gone off at half-cock and blasted two people with a shotgun.'

'Without a body, it would have been a bugger to prove, anyway,' said Bugsy. 'It seems to me that the only thing we could charge Zizi with is attempted blackmail, and since the target is dead and can't confirm the charge, the CPS probably wouldn't look at it. No money changed hands and she has a good brief.'

'Are we all thinking we should let her off with a caution?' suggested Jack.

Velma agreed. 'It must be punishment enough knowing that because you did something foolish, your dearest friend lost her life. I think she'll need counselling.'

When Jack cautioned Zizi, read her the riot act, told her not to do anything similar in the future and to think herself lucky that she was free to go, she burst into a fresh torrent of tears and had to be led away.

CHAPTER TWENTY-SIX

One month later

When Roger Goodman didn't turn up to run the Richington Youth Project, nor to enable all the other activities that took place in the community hall, the committee appointed a replacement caretaker. The lady lived in one of the adjacent bungalows and was within easy reach to unlock doors and provide any other services that were required. However, the lady in question declared she would only oversee what she described as 'proper community pursuits', such as the tea dances, bingo and coffee mornings. She wanted nothing to do with noisy, boisterous teenagers and their loud Saturday nights, which she strongly suspected involved strong drink and drugs and God knows what else – despite having no evidence to prove it. This meant that if nobody took it on, the project would have to close down.

One of the older lads, who fancied himself as something of a budding entrepreneur, called an ad hoc meeting of all the disappointed regulars on the following Saturday. He climbed up onto the stage and addressed the complaining throng. 'Shut up a minute, you lot, I've had an idea. Why don't we run it ourselves? It doesn't look like Roger's coming back from wherever he's gone, but he taught us all we need to know about running this project. We could manage it as a kind of cooperative, with groups of us having responsibility for different activities. What do you say?'

'Do you really think we could do it?' asked a girl.

'Course we could,' added a lad who'd been getting the hang of computer programming and didn't want to stop. 'I'm sure we could persuade the right volunteers to carry on coaching us.'

And thus, the Richington Youth Cooperative was born and became a lasting tribute to Roger Goodman's commitment and enterprise. Their self-styled mission statement declared them to be "an autonomous association of young persons, united voluntarily to meet their common economic, social and cultural needs and aspirations, through a jointly owned and democratically controlled enterprise". It had been drafted by the aspiring young journo who produced the newsletter and saw herself as the future editor of one of the nationals.

At the next dance, the music was provided by *Best in Class* who, thanks to the mentoring of the much-mourned Rocking Robbo, had succeeded in attracting the attention of an agent and were about to release their first album. It was dedicated to Brian and called *Absent Friends*.

* * *

Zizi Starr had reduced the price of Oak Lodge for a quick sale. There was no way she could ever have lived there herself. Whenever she unlocked the front door and went in she imagined she could smell blood, despite having had it professionally cleaned. But, worse than the smell, she could still see the dead body of her best friend slumped halfway up the stairs and peppered with gunshots. The image of Brian with his head blown off haunted her activities in the shop by day, and her fitful dreams at night, when his headless, blood-soaked body would come lurching towards her, like a scene from an old horror movie. The Galaxy Boutique had sold very quickly to a couple of her friends in the trade, who knew a successful business when they saw one.

Living alone without Allegra as friend, confidante and soulmate was intolerable and Zizi couldn't foresee a time when that feeling would go away. She had finally decided that her only future, if she was to live anything approaching a peaceful life, was to join a commune. She had searched online until she found it — Eden Manor, a three-storey Victorian house in the country. Once a children's home, it had been taken over by a group of like-minded people, disillusioned by the misfortunes that life had dished out to them and who had come together for the collective good. It was not, Zizi had established, some kind of hippy crash pad where nobody washed and everybody smelled of patchouli to disguise more suspicious odours. It was a genuine house of solace where she felt she might, one day, heal.

* * *

Jack was washing his hands at the sink in the kitchen.

'I wish you wouldn't do that,' scolded Corrie. 'We have a perfectly serviceable cloakroom, and in case you've forgotten, it's just inside the front door.'

'I know, my little food processor, but I'd rather do it here, where I can feast my eyes on your loveliness and smell the delicious meal that I know you're cooking for us.'

'Do you know what you're full of?' asked Corrie.

'Yes, but I'm too much of a gentleman to say it.' He tried to peer through the glass of the oven door. 'Will it go with red or white wine?'

'Either. Nobody bothers with all that these days. They drink what they like.' She paused. 'Did you know that Mallory's house has been sold?'

'Yes, Bugsy told me. Apparently, his Iris saw her leaving for the last time and she didn't give the place a backward glance, just got into the taxi and left.'

'I think if it had been me, after all she's been through in that ghastly house, I'd have been inclined to make an appropriate gesture.' She took the navarin of lamb out of the oven.

'What — you mean like a two-fingered salute?'

'No, I was thinking of something more meaningful, like breaking all the windows. But I guess that would have been melodrama over common sense. What do you want with this?'

'Chips.'

'But there's gravy.'

'I know. I just fancy chips.'

'Speaking of chips, Ted Barker has been buying a lot of takeaway meals from Corrie's Kitchen over the last few weeks. He told Carlene that since Kirsty's funeral, Mary spends most of her time sitting by the rowan tree in Little Bloomer, rather than by her daughter's grave in the churchyard. He doesn't think she's going to recover anytime soon, so he's putting the farm up for sale. Without Mary and Josh, he can't run it on his own. He hopes that once Mary no longer has access to the field, she may start to improve. That farm has been in the Jackson family for generations. It's so sad.'

'I agree. This whole case and its ripple effect has resulted in upheaval to lots of people's lives. Parnell & Parnell has been absorbed into another, bigger law firm, the exotic Zizi Starr has packed her crystal ball and shimmered away, and Norman Parsloe told me that Constable Walker has left the police.'

'Yes, I know. He's left the family home, too. Tracy Walker packed his bag for him and put it outside on the pavement. He's living in a bedsit down the lower end of Richington High Street. According to Tracy, who comes into Corrie's Kitchen for pizza for the children's teas, Wayne is drinking heavily. She has no sympathy. It seems she offered him a second chance for the sake of the kiddies, but he said he couldn't possibly go back to her after his passionate love affair with the wonderful Allegra, so the divorce is still going through.'

'Stupid bloke.' Jack took the chips, which Corrie had served in a bowl on the side, and emptied them onto his lamb casserole. 'He should have taken his punishment like Nigel the Knob. What's a broken nose compared to a life without being able to watch his kids growing up?'

Corrie poured the wine, trying not to watch as Jack mashed his chips into the carefully prepared navarin jus. 'Did you know George Garwood is expecting a knighthood?'

'What?' Jack almost choked. 'Who told you that?'

'Cynthia. She's already having headed notepaper printed with "Lady Cynthia Garwood".'

'Why? No one writes letters these days.'

'Cynthia does. She leaves threatening notes for the binmen when they drop lobster shells on her begonias.' Corrie laughed. 'I think it's a hoot.'

'No it bloody well isn't! Imagine having to call the old man "Sir George" every time he struts into the incident room!'

Corrie giggled. 'Bugsy will have to learn to curtsey.'

'I'll tell him.'

'But don't start to panic, yet. Apparently, George needs a minimum of two letters of support for the nomination and one of them was going to be from Felix Barrington.'

'Ah.' Jack relaxed and poured another glass of wine. 'Well, that's never going to happen, is it?'

* * *

The meeting of the Friends of the Fungus was agog with anticipation. One of the members had set up a wildlife camera at the spot where the octopus stinkhorn was due to make an appearance. After hours of fruitless recording, it finally emerged. They watched, enthralled, as the young, pink Devil's Fingers erupted from the egg, forming seven elongated arms. At first erect and joined at the top, they slowly unfolded and spread out like a starfish to reveal a red interior covered in dark green, spore-filled slime. It could have been an alien from a horror movie. Watching it on a big screen, they were spared the smell of putrid, rotting flesh.

Such a creature seemed entirely appropriate in a place like the Kings Copse, which for some two years had been the resting place of a rotting human corpse. Although it was still a fetid, dank and dingy place hidden away in a secluded corner of the forest where the sunlight never penetrated, it had become a kind of mecca for mycologists, who came from all over the country. It was not only the habitat of *Clathrus archeri* but all kinds of rare and interesting fungi. This had somehow transformed it into a site of enlightenment and life instead of a place of darkness and death.

CHAPTER TWENTY-SEVEN

The letter was addressed to Inspector Jack Dawes, Murder Investigation Team. It was handed to Sergeant Parsloe on the desk by a young clerk from the law firm that had subsumed Parnell & Parnell, who knew nothing about it except that it had been held by them for some weeks, with strict instructions from the client that it should not be delivered until that date. They had heard nothing from the client since and were unaware of her whereabouts, should a reply be forthcoming.

Norman handed it over. 'Letter for you, Jack. I questioned the lad who brought it in, but he didn't seem to know anything about it.'

Jack examined the envelope. It was handwritten, something of a curiosity in a world of emails and texts. He took a paper knife, carefully slit it open and extracted the letter.

Dear Inspector Dawes.
I am sending you my belated statement in the interests of accuracy and resolution, and also because I need you to know the truth of what happened on that fateful night in the Kings Copse.

It was around midnight and I had been asleep when I heard Felix's car screech into the drive at some speed. It woke the dogs, who began to bark. I got dressed and went outside. I knew something was wrong because he had just abandoned the Range Rover with the door open instead of parking it neatly parallel to mine, as he usually did. I looked inside and there was a lot of blood on the driving seat and a trail down the drive leading to the gate of the Kings Copse. I thought Felix had had an accident. The dogs picked up the scent and ran off. I followed them.

Felix was sitting on the ground in the copse, drinking whiskey from a bottle that was almost empty. His shotgun was lying beside him, with two spent cartridges sticking out of the chamber. He was covered in blood. I asked him what he'd done. He was very drunk and his speech was slurred but I made out the words, 'put a stop to the Parnell bitch' and 'taught her a lesson, poking her nose in'. I was horrified. I thought he'd found out that Allegra was acting for me in the divorce and killed her. I told him I was going back to the house to call the police.

He said "Oh, no you're not", and as I turned away, he struggled unsteadily to his feet and grabbed me round the neck. We both fell down. I screamed and the dogs went for him, snapping and snarling. He let me go and kicked them, viciously, and they yelped in pain.

That, Inspector, was the last straw, the culmination of years of abuse and unhappiness that I had put up with because we were married and I mistakenly believed I had no choice, but I would not tolerate cruelty to my dogs. Felix was staggering, very drunk and no doubt shocked at what he'd done. I pushed him, hard, and he fell onto his back. With strength I didn't know I possessed, I knelt on his chest, put my hands around his throat and squeezed with all my might. He struggled briefly but he was a bony, ineffectual little man and he soon stopped moving. I believed I had killed him and I took the dogs and ran back to the house.

It was at this point that I turned to a dear friend for help. I do not propose to name him here but his identity will, by now, be clear to you. He immediately came to my aid, instructing me to wash off any traces of blood from myself *and the dogs and to go to bed. He said he would deal with everything. I later discovered that he went down to the copse and found Felix unconscious but still with a pulse. I had not been strong enough to strangle him. My friend took the rope from Felix's car, put the noose around his neck and strung him up to a tree to make it look like suicide, which was where you eventually discovered his body. I was shocked when you told me, because I thought I'd choked him to death. But hanging was a more fitting end to an evil, cruel, perverted little man who'd never had a kind thought or done a good deed in his worthless life.*

My friend put the car away in the garage and cleaned up the trail of blood to the house. This enabled me to tell you that I believed Felix to be in town with his prostitutes, and that was why I hadn't looked for him when he hadn't returned home. Later, I heard on the news that Allegra Parnell and her husband had been shot and I knew, then, what Felix had done. It wasn't until much later that I found out it wasn't because of the divorce but because of the terrible crime he had committed two years ago.

So there you have it, Inspector — my confession, and I admit to being unrepentant. By the time you read this, my companion and I will be touring the United States and after that, the Middle East and beyond. Please thank Corrie for her kindness and I wish you both all the happiness in your relationship that I have finally found in mine.

Yours sincerely,
Mallory Barrington.

Jack passed the letter to Clive. 'Scan that, please, and email it to the team. Everyone needs to read it.'

* * *

'What now, guv?' Bugsy asked.

Jack had been silent for some time, deep in thought. He was thinking how very astute Corrie had been about this case and how he should listen to her more often. She'd been right about Allegra being killed because of something she'd found out and that it was someone other than her who had been attempting to blackmail Barrington. She'd spotted the liaison between Mallory and Roger that went far beyond colleagues on the charity committee circuit and he remembered, with clarity, when she had said that if Barrington had been her husband, she wouldn't have waited for him to hang himself, she'd have choked the life out of him herself.

'It explains the bruises on his chest and the dog bites,' said Aled.

'And Aled and Velma were right about Barrington's death not being a suicide,' added Mitch. 'Roger Goodman staged it.'

'That poor woman,' said Gemma. 'We're not going after them, are we, sir? I know a bit about extradition from the US and it's a long and complicated process.'

'And we'd have to find them, first,' said Bugsy. 'It's a big place and it sounds from the letter as if they're planning to tour beyond the States. They must have some kind of camper van.'

Clive looked up from his screen. 'I tried to track them, sir, but the trail went cold after they landed at the John F Kennedy International Airport, New York, a month ago. No hotel bookings, no hire car, their bank accounts and credit cards were all closed down before they left. They must have put their money in offshore accounts, probably under different names. I'll keep searching, but they've covered themselves very well.'

'Offshore accounts aren't necessarily illegal but using them to hide money is,' said Gemma.

Before Jack could express an opinion, the door opened and Chief Superintendent Garwood strode in. As head of the MIT, the letter had appeared on his screen, too. 'What are you planning to do about this, Inspector?'

Jack was guarded. 'What would you advise, sir?'

Garwood blustered a bit before answering, which he invariably did when he suspected he might be on shaky ground. 'Technically, they're both guilty of murder by joint enterprise, but the coroner was satisfied it was suicide. Frankly, Dawes, I can't see what good it would do to try and charge them at this stage, even if we knew where they were.'

'Extradition would be very expensive, sir,' said Gemma. 'A serious drain on taxpayers' money.'

Garwood cleared his throat, anxiously. 'The public aren't keen on the police backtracking. There'd be awkward questions about why we didn't get it right in the first place.' He had a sudden thought. 'Has Sir Barnaby seen this?'

'Not yet, sir.' Jack knew what was coming.

'Probably better if he doesn't. No point in troubling him with what is to all intents and purposes a closed case.' He lowered his voice. 'Whatever you do, don't let the press get hold of it.' He could picture his knighthood going right down the proverbial. He strutted out, muttering to himself.

'What I don't understand,' said Aled, 'is why Mrs Barrington wrote that letter in the first place. She and Roger Goodman are home free. Other than raising a few eyebrows about why they'd disappeared at the same time, nobody would have questioned it. Her husband was dead and she'd moved away for a new start. It was perfectly reasonable.'

'Conscience, Aled,' answered Velma. 'Mallory Barrington had a strong personal sense of moral conduct and character, a feeling of obligation to do the right thing, which is why she stayed in that terrible marriage as long as she did. She couldn't move on with her life without wiping the slate clean, and writing that letter was her way of doing it.'

'You haven't said what you think, sir,' said Gemma. 'I know that upholding the law and protecting the public is a police officer's job — it's why I joined. But there's a philosophical question, a conflict of interests that I can't get straight in my mind. Is it always right to stick to the letter of the law? Must we, as police officers, relentlessly pursue a person to the bitter end for the sake of principles and procedure, no matter how pointless and cruel it seems?'

Jack smiled. 'I was asked this same question a few years ago by Carlene, a young lady who's very dear to me. I'll give you the same answer I gave her. What I've learned as a police officer, Gemma, is that for the sake of compassion and humanity, it's sometimes necessary to jam a stick in the wheels of justice. Does that answer your question?'

She beamed. 'Perfectly, sir. Thank you.'

THE END

Thank you for reading this book.

If you enjoyed it please leave feedback on Amazon or Goodreads, and if there is anything we missed or you have a question about, then please get in touch. We appreciate you choosing our book.

Founded in 2014 in Shoreditch, London, we at Joffe Books pride ourselves on our history of innovative publishing. We were thrilled to be shortlisted for Independent Publisher of the Year at the British Book Awards.

www.joffebooks.com

We're very grateful to eagle-eyed readers who take the time to contact us. Please send any errors you find to corrections@joffebooks.com. We'll get them fixed ASAP.

Milton Keynes UK
Ingram Content Group UK Ltd.
UKHW041446090724
445399UK00023B/196